French Dictionary

Aladdin Books
Macmillan Publishing Company
New York

Maxwell Macmillan Canada
Toronto

Maxwell Macmillan International
New York   Oxford   Singapore   Sydney

Aladdin Books
Macmillan Publishing Company
866 Third Avenue
New York, NY 10022

Maxwell Macmillan Canada, Inc.
1200 Eglinton Avenue East
Suite 200
Don Mills, Ontario M3C 3N1

Macmillan Publishing Company is part of the Maxwell Communication Group of
Companies.

Illustrations by Cathy Beylon/Evelyne Johnson Associates

First Aladdin Books edition 1992

Printed in the United States of America

10 9 8 7 6 5 4 3 2 1

Library of Congress Cataloging-in-Publication Data

Berlitz Jr. French dictionary — 1st ed.
p.   cm.
Summary: Gives the French equivalent of more than 500 English
words and uses each of them in a sentence in the appropriate
language.
ISBN 0-689-71539-0
1. English language—Dictionaries—French—Juvenile literature.
2. French language—Dictionaries, Juvenile. [1. English language—
Dictionaries—French. 2. French language materials—Bilingual.]
I. Berlitz Schools of Languages of America. II. Title: Berlitz
Junior French dictionary. III. Title: French dictionary.
PC2629.B47 1992
443′.21—dc20   91-40123

To the parent:

Learning a foreign language is one of the best ways to expand your child's horizons. It immediately exposes him or her to a foreign culture—especially important at a time when the world is more of a "global village" than ever before.

This *Berlitz Jr.* dictionary is the first Berlitz publication of its kind for children. The text has been approved by foreign-language experts and meets the Berlitz standard of quality. Teddy Berlitz and his friends bring French to life by introducing simple words and phrases, without the need for grammatical drills or exercises.

The vocabulary has been chosen based on frequency lists, content of beginning language courses, and the natural interests of children. This controlled vocabulary makes it a perfect reference for beginning students and their parents. It is also an ideal companion to the *Berlitz Jr.* book-and-cassette kit.

Entries have been arranged alphabetically in English. Each word is followed by its French counterpart and an English definition. An example sentence in both French and English shows the word in context and is accompanied by a vivid illustration so children can associate pictures with meanings. Special illustrated "theme pages" reinforce the most basic vocabulary, such as numbers, colors, and common household words.

Every child has the ability to learn a foreign language, and *Berlitz Jr.* helps children to tap that potential. Enjoy sharing this dictionary—and watching your child's world grow.

Berlitz Publishing Company

AFRAID (TO BE): PEUR (AVOIR)

The feeling you have when you are frightened or scared.

The small mouse is afraid of the big cat.
La petite souris a peur du gros chat.

AFTERNOON: APRÈS-MIDI

Afternoon is the part of the day between noon and nighttime.

Every afternoon Joey takes a nap.
L'après-midi Jacques fait la sieste.

AIRPLANE: AVION

Airplanes are big machines that can fly.

Johnny flies everywhere in his small, red airplane.
Jean vole partout dans son petit avion rouge.

AIRPORT: AÉROPORT

Airplanes land and take off at the airport.

Susan is leaving for vacation from the airport.
Suzanne depart pour ses vacances de l'aéroport.

AMERICAN: AMÉRICAIN

An American is a person who lives in the United States of America.

Teddy is proud to be an American.
Teddy est fier d'être américain.

AND: ET

And means also. We use the word *and* to join words and phrases.

Here are a proud, green rooster and a plump, brown hen.
Voici un fier coq vert et une grosse poule marron.

ANGRY: EN COLÈRE

You feel angry when you are unhappy and upset at someone or something.

Tim the Gorilla is very angry.
Le gorille Tim est très en colère.

ANIMAL: ANIMAL

An animal is any living thing that is not a plant.

Dogs, bees, and frogs are all animals.
Les chiens, les abeilles, et les grenouilles sont des animaux.

ANSWER: RÉPONDRE

When you answer someone, you reply to a question, call, or letter.

Teddy answers the teacher's question.
Teddy répond à la question de sa maîtresse.

ANT: FOURMI

Ants are small, fast insects that live in the ground.

Tina the Ant works hard all summer long.
La fourmi Tina travaille dur pendant tout l'été.

APPLE: POMME

An apple is a crispy fruit that can be red, yellow, or green.

This apple is red and very shiny.
Cette pomme est rouge et très luisante.

APRIL: AVRIL

April is the fourth month of the year.

April showers bring May flowers.
Les averses d'avril amènent les fleurs du mois de mai.

ARAB: ARABE

An Arab is a person from Arabia.
Un arabe est originaire d'Arabie.

ARM: BRAS

Your arm connects your shoulder to your wrist.

This gorilla has very long arms.
Ce gorille a des bras très longs.

ASK: DEMANDER

Ask a question if you want to know the answer.

Joey asks the policeman the way to his friend William's house.

Jacques demande au policier le chemin de la maison de son ami Guillaume.

ASTRONAUT: ASTRONAUTE

An astronaut is a person who travels to outer space.

This astronaut is exploring the moon.
Cet astronaute explore la lune.

AUGUST: AOÛT

August is the seventh month of the year.

It's very hot in August, and we eat lots of ice cream.
En août, il fait très chaud, et nous mangeons beaucoup de glace.

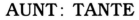

AUNT: TANTE

Your aunt is the sister of your father or your mother.
Ta tante est la soeur de ton père ou de ta mère.

BAD: MÉCHANT

Bad is the opposite of good. When people are being bad, they are doing something naughty.

This little monster is very bad.
Ce petit monstre est très méchant.

BAG: SAC

A bag is a sack to carry things in.

Father Bear, Mother Bear, and Teddy are carrying bags of groceries.
Papa Ours, Maman Ours, et Teddy portent tous des sacs de victuailles.

BALL: BALLE

A ball is a round object that is used in many kinds of games.

Teddy's favorite ball is red, white, and blue.
La balle préférée de Teddy est rouge, blanche, et bleue.

BANANA: BANANE

A banana is a sweet, yellow fruit.

Gorillas really like bananas.
Les gorilles aiment beaucoup les bananes.

BARBER: COIFFEUR

A barber cuts your hair when it's too long.

Barber Bob cuts Mr. Bear's hair.
Le coiffeur Robert coupe les cheveux de Monsieur Ours.

BASKETBALL: BASKET-BALL

Basketball is a fast game played with a ball and by two teams.

Jimmy the Giraffe is the tallest player on his basketball team.

La girafe Jim est le joueur le plus grand de cette équipe de basket-ball.

BAT: BATTE

A bat is a strong stick that is used to hit a baseball.

A famous baseball player autographed Teddy's bat.

Un fameux joueur de base-ball a signé la batte de Teddy.

BE: ÊTRE

To be means to exist.

Teddy writes the verb *to be* on a piece of paper.

Teddy écrit le verbe être *sur sa feuille de papier.*

BEACH: PLAGE

A beach is a sandy or rocky area by the ocean or a lake.

Teddy likes to build sand castles at the beach in summer.

Teddy aime construire des châteaux de sable à la plage en été.

BEAN: HARICOT

A bean is a seed that we eat as a vegetable.

Lisa has left some red and green beans on her plate.

Lisa a laissé des haricots verts et rouges sur son assiette.

6

BEAR: OURS

A bear is a big animal covered with thick fur.

Polar bears are white, and they like to play in the snow.
Les ours polaires sont blancs, et ils aiment jouer dans la neige.

BEAUTIFUL: BEAU (BELLE)

When something is beautiful, it is pretty to look at.

Rita thinks she is very beautiful.
Rita se croit très belle.

BED: LIT

A bed is a place to sleep when you're tired.

Teddy's big, soft bed has a warm, red blanket.
Le grand lit doux de Teddy a une couverture rouge et chaude.

BEE: ABEILLE

A bee is an insect that makes honey.

Bees are flying around the flowers on Dora's hat.
Les abeilles volent au mileu des fleurs du chapeau de Dora.

BEFORE: AVANT

Before means earlier in time.

Leo the Lion arrived at the theater before the movie began.

Le lion Léo est arrivé au théâtre avant le début du film.

BEHIND: DERRIÈRE

Behind means in back of.

The three little bears walk behind Mama Bear.

Les trois oursons marchent derrière Maman Ours.

BELT: CEINTURE

You wear a belt around your waist to hold up your pants or skirt.

This is Papa Bear's favorite leather belt.
Cette ceinture de cuir est la préférée de papa Ours.

BICYCLE: BICYCLETTE

A bicycle has two wheels, handlebars, and pedals, and is fun to ride.

Teddy has just fallen off his red bicycle.
Teddy vient de tomber de sa bicyclette rouge.

BIG : GRAND

Big is the opposite of small. It means large.

Joey is a very big elephant who went to his small friend Gus's wedding.

Jacques est un très grand éléphant qui est allé au mariage de Gus, son très petit ami.

BIRD : OISEAU

A bird is an animal with wings, feathers, and a beak.

Chickens, penguins, and ducks are birds.

Les poulets, les pingouins, et les canards sont des oiseaux.

BIRTHDAY : ANNIVERSAIRE

Your birthday is the day when you were born. You celebrate it every year.

Today is Teddy's birthday. He is six years old.

Aujourd'hui c'est l'anniversaire de Teddy. Il a six ans.

BLACK : NOIR

Black is a very dark color.

Marie spilled black ink on her paper.

Marie a versé de l'encre noire sur son papier.

BLACKBOARD : TABLEAU NOIR

At school, you write on the blackboard with a piece of chalk.

Teddy is doing a sum on the blackboard.

Teddy fait une addition au tableau noir.

BLANKET: COUVERTURE

A blanket is a cover that keeps you warm in bed.

Our little friends are covering themselves with a big, brown blanket.
Nos petits amis se couvrent d'une grande couverture marron.

BLOND: BLOND

Blond hair is yellow or gold in color.

Dodo's hair is very blond.
Les cheveux de Dodo sont très blonds.

BLUE: BLEU

Blue is the color of the sky when it's sunny.

Jane's eyes are as blue as the sky.
Les yeux de Jeanne sont aussi bleus que le ciel.

BOAT: BARQUE

A boat is used to travel on water.

Cricket loves to row in his little boat.
Criquet aime ramer dans sa petite barque.

BOOK: LIVRE

A book has pages with words and pictures on them for people to read.

Teddy's teacher is showing the class a very nice picture book.
La maîtresse de Teddy montre à la classe un très joli livre de dessins.

BOTTLE: BOUTEILLE

A bottle is used to hold liquids.

Joey is pouring a bottle of milk.
Jacques verse une bouteille du lait.

BOX: BOÎTE

A box is a container used to hold things.

Matthew wants to put the candy into one of these boxes.
Mathieu veut mettre le bonbon dans une des boîtes.

BOY: GARÇON

A boy is a child who will be a man one day.

All these boys are on the same baseball team.
Tous ces garçons sont dans la même équipe de base-ball.

BRANCH: BRANCHE

A branch is the part of a tree that grows from the trunk and has leaves.

Our friend Sherlock is sawing off a branch, and I'm afraid he'll fall along with it.
Notre ami Sherlock scie une branche, et j'ai peur qu'il tombe avec elle.

BRAVE: COURAGEUX

A brave person is someone who isn't afraid.

The ship's captain is very brave.
Le capitaine de ce navire est très courageux.

BREAD: PAIN

Bread is a baked food that is usually made from flour, yeast, and milk.

With these two slices of bread, Teddy is going to make a sandwich.
Avec ces deux tranches de pain, Teddy va se faire un sandwich.

BREAKFAST: PETIT DÉJEUNER

Breakfast is the first meal of the day.

Pete the Octopus always enjoys his breakfast.
La pieuvre Pierre aime toujours son petit déjeuner.

BRIDGE: PONT

A bridge is a roadway that is built across water.

Theo's small paper boat sails under the stone bridge.
La petite barque de papier de Théo passe sous la pont de pierre.

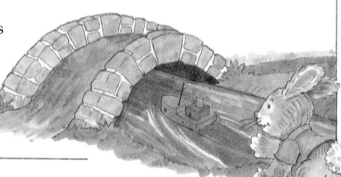

BROTHER: FRÈRE

Your brother has the same mother and same father as you do.

Steven's big brother's name is Anthony.
Le frère aîne d'Étienne s'appelle Antoine.

BROWN: MARRON

Brown is the color of chocolate and toasted coffee beans.

This pony is brown, but its mane and tail are white.
Ce petit cheval est marron, mais sa crinière et sa queue sont blanches.

BUS: AUTOBUS

A bus is a large vehicle used to transport people.

This red double-decker bus is crowded today.
Cet autobus rouge à deux étages est bondé aujourd'hui.

BUTTERFLY: PAPILLON

A butterfly is an insect with four brightly colored wings.

This beautifully colored butterfly flies lightly everywhere.
Ce papillon aux couleurs magnifiques vole légèrement un peu partout.

BUTTON: BOUTON

A button is a small object that is used to fasten clothes.

Here are three different buttons.
Voici trois boutons différents.

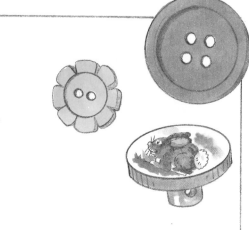

BUY: ACHETER

When you buy something, you pay money for it.

Mrs. Rabbit has gone to the market to buy some pears.
Madame Lapin est allée au marché pour acheter des poires.

CAKE: GÂTEAU

A cake is a sweet food that is baked in an oven.

Teddy has just eaten a big piece of his favorite cake.
Teddy vient de manger un grand morceau de son gâteau préféré.

CALL: APPELER

When you want to talk to someone who is not near you, you call him.

Porcupine is using a pink phone to call his friend.
Porc-épic utilise un téléphone rose pour appeler son ami.

14

CAMEL: CHAMEAU

A camel is a four-legged animal that lives in the desert.

This camel lives in the Sahara and can go days without drinking any water.

Ce chameau vit dans le désert du Sahara et peut rester des jours sans boire d'eau.

CAMERA: APPAREIL

A camera is used to take photographs or movies.

Teddy's father takes pictures with this new camera.

Le père de Teddy fait des photos avec ce nouvel appareil.

CAP: CASQUETTE

A cap is a small, soft hat.

These baseball players are wearing matching caps.

Ces joueurs de base-ball portent des casquettes assorties.

CAR: AUTOMOBILE

A car is a four-wheeled vehicle with a motor that runs on gas.

Joey's small, green car has a flat tire.

La petite automobile verte de Jacques a un pneu dégonflé.

CARPET: TAPIS

A carpet is a large rug that covers the floor.

Arthur the Crocodile has just bought a flying carpet.

Le crocodile Arthur vient d'acheter un tapis volant.

CARROT: CAROTTE

Carrots are crispy, orange vegetables that grow in the ground.

This must be the biggest carrot ever grown.

Ce doit être la plus grosse carotte jamais cultivée.

CARTOONS: DESSINS ANIMÉS

A cartoon is a picture that makes you laugh.

In the afternoon we sometimes watch cartoons on televison.

L'après-midi nous regardons quelquefois les dessins animés à la télévision.

CASTLE: CHÂTEAU

A castle is a large building where princes and princesses used to live.

Once upon a time Merlin the Magician lived in this castle.

Il était une fois le magicien Merlin qui vivait dans ce château.

CAT: CHAT

A cat is a small animal with soft fur and whiskers.

This cat is smiling because it has just seen a mouse.
Ce chat sourit car il vient de voir une souris.

CATERPILLAR: CHENILLE

A caterpillar is an insect that looks like a hairy green worm. Caterpillars turn into butterflies or moths.

How many rollerskates does this caterpillar need?
De combien de patins à roulettes cette chenille a-t-elle besoin?

CHAIR: CHAISE

A chair is a piece of furniture that you sit on.

This chair is from Teddy's bedroom.
Cette chaise est de la chambre de Teddy.

CHEESE: FROMAGE

Cheese is a food made from milk.

Cheese is a mouse's favorite food.
Le fromage est la nourriture préférée d'une souris.

CHILD (CHILDREN): ENFANT(S)

A child is a young boy or girl.

Teddy and his friends Anne and Matt are still children.

Teddy et ses amis Anne et Mathieu sont encore des enfants.

CHOCOLATE: CHOCOLAT

Chocolate is a food used to make candy. It is usually sweet and brown.

This chocolate bar is for Teddy and his friends.

Cette tablette de chocolat est pour Teddy et ses amis.

CHRISTMAS: NOËL

Christmas is a Christian holiday that is celebrated on December 25.

Teddy puts the star on the top of the Christmas tree.

Teddy place l'étoile au sommet de l'arbre de Noël.

CIRCLE: CERCLE

A circle is a perfectly round shape.

The full moon is a circle.

La pleine lune est un cercle.

CIRCUS: CIRQUE

A circus is a traveling show with performing animals, clowns, and acrobats.

These clowns entertain the children at the circus.

Ces clowns amusent les enfants au cirque.

CLASSROOM: SALLE DE CLASSE

A classroom is a room where you and your schoolmates have lessons.

Today is Sunday, so Teddy's classroom is empty and quiet.

Aujourd'hui c'est dimanche, donc la salle de classe de Teddy est vide et silencieuse.

CLEAN: PROPRE

When something is clean, it does not have dirt on it.

Mrs. Rabbit is looking at her wash to see if it's really clean.

Madame Lapin regarde sa lessive pour voir si elle est vraiment propre.

CLOCK: HORLOGE

The numbers on the clock tell you what time it is.

It's midnight on the old tower clock.

Il est minuit à la vieille horloge de la tour.

CLOSED: FERMÉ

When something is not open, it's closed.

The window in Teddy's bedroom is now closed.

La fenêtre de la chambre de Teddy est maintenant fermée.

CLOSET: PLACARD

A closet is a small room used for storing things.

Teddy hangs up his jacket in the closet.
Teddy pend sa jaquette dans le placard.

CLOUD: NUAGE

A cloud is a cluster of tiny water drops that float in the sky.

Small, soft, white clouds float in the sky.
De petits nuages blancs et doux flottent dans le ciel.

COAT: MANTEAU

A coat is a piece of clothing that is worn outside in winter.

William is trying on a nice blue coat, but it's too big for him.
Guillaume essaye un joli manteau bleu, mais il est trop grand pour lui.

COFFEE: CAFÉ

Coffee is a hot drink for grown-ups.

This cup of piping hot coffee is for Teddy's father.
Cette tasse de café chaud est pour le père de Teddy.

COLD: FROID

Cold is the opposite of hot. Ice cream, snow, and winter are all cold things.

Andy is cold because he forgot his coat.
André a froid parce qu'il a oublié son manteau.

COLOR: COULEUR

If colors didn't exist, everything would be just black, white, and gray.
Si les couleurs n'existaient pas, tout serait noir, blanc, et gris.

COMB: PEIGNE

You use a comb to fix your hair.

Leo is fixing his beautiful mane with a big comb.
Léo coiffe sa jolie crinière avec un grand peigne.

COMPUTER: ORDINATEUR

A computer is a special machine that we can use to play or to work with.

Teddy's parents bought him a new computer.
Les parents de Teddy lui ont acheté un nouvel ordinateur.

CONE: CÔNE

A cone is a shape with a circular base and a pointed top.

Un cône a une base circulaire et un dessus pointu.

COOK: FAIRE CUIRE

Cook means to prepare food for eating.

Teddy and his father are cooking dinner.
Teddy et son père font cuire le dîner.

COOKIE: BISCUIT

Cookies are flat, sweet foods that taste good with a big glass of cold milk.

This big blue box is full of delicious cookies.
Cette grande boîte bleue est pleine de biscuits délicieux.

COPY: COPIER

When you copy something, you make it just like something else.

Joey shouldn't copy the answers from Andy's homework.
Jacques ne devrait pas copier les réponses des devoirs de André.

COUNT: COMPTER

When you count, you say the numbers in order.

Amanda can count to ten on her fingers.
Amanda peut compter jusqu'à dix sur ses doigts.

COUNTRY: PAYS

A country is a land with its own government.

The United States, Mexico, and Japan are all countries.
Les États-Unis, le Mexique, et le Japon sont tous des pays.

COWBOY: COWBOY

A cowboy rides a horse and takes care of cattle on a ranch.

Teddy dressed up like a cowboy for Halloween.
Teddy a mis un costume de cowboy pour Halloween.

CROCODILE: CROCODILE

A crocodile is a reptile with sharp teeth that lives in swamps.

Arthur is a friendly crocodile who lives in Florida.
Arthur est un crocodile sympathique qui vit en Floride.

CROSS: TRAVERSER

When you cross something, you go from one side of it to the other.

These three friends always cross the street carefully.
Ces trois amis traversent toujours la rue prudemment.

CRY: PLEURER

You cry when you are sad, and tears come out of your eyes.

Patty the Octopus is crying because her doll is broken.
La pieuvre Pierrette pleure parce que sa poupée est cassée.

23

CUP: TASSE

You drink hot liquids from a cup.

Teddy uses this big, white cup to drink his hot chocolate in the morning.
Teddy utilise cette grande tasse blanche pour boire son chocolat chaud le matin.

CUPBOARD: ARMOIRE

A cupboard is a small cabinet used for storage.

The toys are in the cupboard.
Les jouets sont dans l'armoire.

CUT: COUPER

You cut things into pieces with a knife or scissors.

Teddy likes to cut shapes out of paper.
Teddy aime couper des formes en papier.

DADDY: PAPA

Young children call their fathers Daddy.

Teddy's daddy loves him very much.
Le papa de Teddy l'aime beaucoup.

DANCE: DANSER

To dance is to move your body to music.

Cricket is always happy when he can dance.
Criquet est toujours content quand il peut danser.

DANGER: DANGER

Danger means that something could hurt or harm you.

If you don't obey the danger sign, your car will go off the cliff.
Si tu n'obéis pas au signal de danger, ton automobile tombera de la falaise.

DAUGHTER: FILLE

A daughter is the female child of two parents.

Teddy's parents have one daughter.
Les parents de Teddy ont une fille.

DAY: JOUR

There are 365 days in one year.

Today is a sunny day.
Aujourd'hui est un jour ensoleillé.

DECEMBER: DÉCEMBRE

December is the twelfth and last month of the year.

Christmas is in December.
Noël est en décembre.

DEER: CERF

A deer is a forest animal with four legs and short fur. Male deer have antlers.

The deer live in the forest.
Les cerf habitent à la forêt.

DENTIST: DENTISTE

A dentist is a doctor who keeps our teeth healthy.

Hippo is very afraid of the dentist.
Hippo a très peur du dentiste.

DESK: PUPITRE

A desk is a table used for writing or reading.

Teddy's book is on the desk.
Le livre de Teddy est sur le pupitre.

DIFFERENT: DIFFÉRENT

When something is different, it is not the same as something else.

The blue sock is different from the red one.
La chaussette bleue est différente de la rouge.

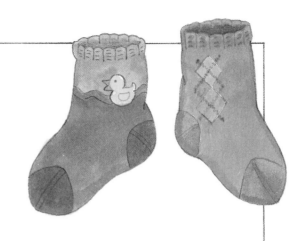

DINNER: DÎNER

Dinner is the last meal of the day.

Joey invited his friends Marie and Cricket to dinner.
Jacques a invité ses amis Marie et Criquet à dîner.

DINOSAUR: DINOSAURE

A dinosaur was an animal that lived millions of years ago.

Dino the Dinosaur has a red flower in his mouth.
Le dinosaure Dino a une fleur rouge à la bouche.

DIRTY: SALE

If something is dirty, it isn't clean.

Teddy is dirty because he has played soccer.
Teddy est sale parce qu'il a joué au football américain.

DOCTOR: DOCTEUR

A doctor is a person who helps sick people get better.

This doctor is going to visit a sick patient.
Ce docteur va visiter un client malade.

DOG: CHIEN

A dog is a four-legged animal that barks.

Bull the Dog looks vicious, but he really isn't.
Le chien Bull semble méchant, mais en réalité il ne l'est pas.

DOLL: POUPÉE

A doll is a toy that looks like a person.

Annie is a pretty rag doll.
Annie est une jolie poupée de chiffon.

DOLPHIN: DAUPHIN

A dolphin is a sea mammal that is very friendly and playful.

Dan the Dolphin can jump through hoops.
Le dauphin Dan peut sauter à travers les anneaux.

DONKEY: ÂNE

A donkey is an animal that looks like a small horse.

David the Donkey refuses to carry baskets full of apples.

L'âne David refuse de porter des paniers pleins de pommes.

DOOR: PORTE

A door is an entrance to a room or a building.

The milkman left two bottles of milk by the door.

Le laitier a laissé deux bouteilles de lait devant la porte.

DOORBELL: SONNETTE

You ring the doorbell to let people know that you're outside.

Toby rings the doorbell.
Tobie utilise la sonnette.

DOWN: BAS

Down is the opposite of up.

Leo skis swiftly to the foot of the hill.
Léo skie rapidement jusqu'en bas de la colline.

DRAWING: DESSIN

A drawing is a picture done with pencils, ink, or crayons.

Teddy is very proud of his drawing.
Teddy est très fier de son dessin.

DRESS: S'HABILLER

To dress means to put on clothes.

Hippo gets dressed to go to school.
Hippo s'habille pour aller à l'école.

DRINK: BOIRE

To drink means to swallow a liquid.

Tom the Tiger likes to drink lemonade when it's hot.
Le tigre Thomas aime boire de la limonade quand il fait chaud.

DRIVE: CONDUIRE

To drive is to operate a car, bus, or truck.

Who is driving this fast red car?
Qui conduit cette voiture rapide et rouge?

DRY: SEC (SÈCHE)

Dry means without water or moisture.

All the clean laundry is dry now.
Toute la lessive propre est sèche maintenant.

DUCK: CANARD

A duck is a bird that swims in water.

The small, yellow duck is learning to swim.
Le petit canard jaune apprend à nager.

EAGLE: AIGLE

An eagle is a large bird with sharp claws and long wings.

The bald eagle is the symbol of the United States.
L'aigle à tête blanche est l'emblême des États-Unis.

EAR: OREILLE

An ear is the part of the body that is used to hear.

Rodney the Rabbit has such long ears!
Le lapin Rodney a de si grandes oreilles!

EARLY: TÔT

Early means before the usual time. It is the opposite of late.

Michael woke up too early this morning.
Michel s'est levé trop tôt ce matin.

EASY CHAIR: FAUTEUIL

An easy chair is a comfortable piece of furniture to sit on.

Hippo's favorite easy chair is green.
Le fauteuil préféré de Hippo est vert.

EAT: MANGER

When you eat, you chew and swallow your food.

This mouse wants to eat the cheese, but the cheese is in the trap.
Cette souris veut manger le fromage, mais le fromage est dans le piège.

EGG: OEUF

Baby chicks hatch from eggs.

This is a fresh, white egg.
C'est un oeuf blanc et frais.

EIGHT: HUIT

Eight is the number after seven and before nine.

Here are eight nuts all in a row.
Voici huit noix côte à côte.

ELEPHANT: ÉLÉPHANT

An elephant is a huge animal that has big ears and a long nose called a trunk.

This friendly elephant works in a circus.
Cet éléphant sympathique travaille dans un cirque.

ENGLISH: ANGLAIS

English is a language that is spoken in England, the United States, and Canada.

Do you speak English?
Parlez-vous anglais?

ENVELOPE: ENVELOPPE

Letters and cards are mailed in envelopes.

This envelope is for a birthday card.
Cette enveloppe est pour une carte d'anniversaire.

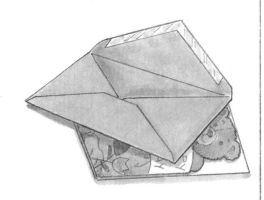

EVENING: SOIR

Evening is the time of day when it starts to get dark.

In the evening our friends watch the sunset.
Le soir nos amis contemplent le coucher de soleil.

EXERCISE: EXERCICE

An exercise is an activity that keeps our bodies healthy.

Mrs. Hippo does her exercises every morning.
Madame Hippo fait ses exercices chaque matin.

EYE: OEIL

An eye is the part of the body that is used to see.

The octopus and the kangaroo both have black eyes.
La pieuvre et le kangourou ont des yeux noirs.

FACE: VISAGE

Your face is the front part of your head.

Teddy's face is reflected in the mirror.
Le visage de Teddy se reflète dans le miroir.

FAIRY: FÉE

A fairy is a make-believe person with magical powers.

All fairies have special magic wands.
Toutes les fées ont des baguettes magiques spéciales.

FAIRY TALE: CONTES DE FÉES

A fairy tale is a story about magical people and their adventures.

"Goldilocks and the Three Bears" is my favorite fairy tale.
Mon conte de fées préféré est "Goldilocks et les trois ours."

FALL: AUTOMNE

Fall is the season before winter, when the days get cool and the leaves fall off the trees.

In fall the children must go back to school.
En automne les enfants doivent retourner à l'école.

FAMILY: FAMILLE

A family includes parents, children, and lots of other relatives.

Teddy's family isn't very big.
La famille de Teddy n'est pas très grande.

FARM: FERME

A farm is a place where animals are raised and crops are grown.

Julia grows corn on her farm.
Julie fait pousser du maïs dans sa ferme.

FAST: RAPIDE

Fast is the opposite of slow. To be fast is to be quick.

I couldn't catch him! He was too fast.
Je n'ai pas pu le rattraper! Il était trop rapide.

FATHER: PÈRE

A father is a man who has one or more children.

Teddy's father has two sons and a daughter.
Le père de Teddy a deux fils et une fille.

FEBRUARY: FÉVRIER

February is the second month of the year.

In February it's cold and there's lots of snow.
En février il fait froid et il y a beaucoup de neige.

FINGER: DOIGT

You have five fingers on each hand.

Theo hurt his finger with the hammer.
Théo s'est blessé au doigt avec le marteau.

FIRE : FEU

A fire is made when something is burning.

In winter there's always a fire in the fireplace.
En hiver il y a toujours du feu dans la cheminée.

FIREFIGHTER : POMPIER

A firefighter is a person who puts out fires.

Bruno the firefighter put out Mr. Crow's cigar.
Le pompier Bruno a éteint le cigare de Monsieur Corbeau.

FISH : POISSON

A fish is an animal with fins and scales that lives in the water.

This big fish loves to swim lazily.
Ce grand poisson aime nager paresseusement.

FISHERMAN : PÊCHEUR

A fisherman is a person who catches fish, for sport or as a job.

Teddy is a good and patient fisherman.
Teddy est un bon pêcheur patient.

FIVE: CINQ

Five is the number that comes after four and before six.

Here are five shiny red apples to eat.
Voici cinq pommes rouges et luisantes à manger.

FLAG: DRAPEAU

A flag is piece of cloth with different colors and designs on it.

Tim is holding his club's flag.
Tim porte le drapeau de son club.

FLOWER: FLEUR

A flower is the brightly colored part of a plant that has petals.

Teddy is watering his favorite flowers.
Teddy arrose ses fleurs préférées.

FLU: GRIPPE

The flu is caused by a virus and makes you feel very sick.

Doggy didn't go to school today because he had the flu.
Doggy n'est pas allé à l'école aujourd'hui parce qu'il avait la grippe.

FLY AWAY: S'ENVOLER

Fly away means to move through the air with wings.

This bird is flying away south for the winter.
L'oiseau s'envole vers le sud en hiver.

FOG: BROUILLARD

Fog is a thick cloud close to the ground.

There's so much fog that Mr. Hound can't see a thing.
Il y a tant de brouillard que Monsieur Limier ne peut rien voir.

FOOT: PIED

The foot is the part of the body at the end of the leg.

Guess who broke his foot playing football?
Devine qui s'est cassé le pied en jouant au football américain?

FORGET: OUBLIER

When you forget, you don't remember to do something.

Teddy forgot to buy orange juice.
Teddy a oublié d'acheter du jus d'oranges.

FOUR: QUATRE

Four is the number that comes after three, but before five.

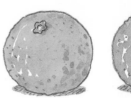

Here are four juicy oranges all in a row.
Voici quatre oranges juteuses côte à côte.

FOX: RENARD

A fox is a bushy-tailed animal with beautiful reddish fur.

Frank is a very friendly fox.
François est un renard très sympathique.

FRENCHMAN: FRANÇAIS

A Frenchman is a native of France.
Un français est originaire de France.

FRIDAY: VENDREDI

Friday is the fifth day of the week.

Rita takes dance classes on Friday.
Rita prend des cours de danse tous les vendredis.

FRIEND: AMI

A friend is someone you like and who likes you, too.

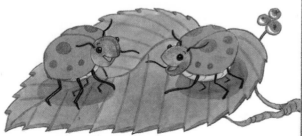

These two ladybugs are very good friends.
Ces deux coccinelles sont de très bonnes amies.

FROG: GRENOUILLE

A frog is an animal that has long hind legs, that croaks, and that can live both in and out of the water.

Frogs love to go swimming.
Les grenouilles aiment nager.

FRUIT: FRUIT

A fruit is the part of a plant that holds the seeds. Apples, cherries, and oranges are all fruits.

Teddy's uncle sells fruit in the market.
L'oncle de Teddy vend des fruits au marché.

FULL: PLEIN

When something is full, it's holding all it can.

This mug is full of soda.
Cette tasse est pleine de soda.

FUNNEL: ENTONNOIR

A funnel is used to pass liquids from one bottle to another.

This funnel is used to fill bottles with oil.
On utilise cet entonnoir pour remplir les bouteilles d'huile.

GARAGE: GARAGE

A garage is a building where cars, buses, or trucks are parked.

There are many cars in this garage.
Il y a beaucoup d'automobiles dans ce garage.

GATE: GRILLE

A gate is an opening in a wall or fence.

Someone hurt himself jumping over the gate.
Quelqu'un a du mal à sauter par-dessus la grille.

GERMAN: ALLEMAND

A German is a native of Germany.
Un allemand est originaire d'Allemagne.

GIRL: FILLE

A girl is a female child.

Teddy's sister, Susan, is a girl.
Suzanne, la soeur de Teddy, est une fille.

GIVE: DONNER

To give means to let someone have something to keep.

Penguin gives flowers to his girlfriend.
Pingouin donne des fleurs à son amie.

GLASS: VERRE

A glass is a container that is used for drinking.

These glasses are very delicate.
Ces verres sont très fins.

GLOVE: GANT

A glove is a piece of clothing to wear on your hand.

Poor Pete the Octopus! He needs so many gloves!
Pauvre Pierre la pieuvre! Il a besoin de tant de gants!

GLUE: COLLE

We use glue to make things stick together.

Teddy has spilled a bottle of glue.
Teddy a versé une bouteille de la colle.

GOAT: CHÈVRE

A goat is an animal with horns and a short, pointed beard.

Goats like to bang against trees with their horns.
Les chèvres aiment secouer les arbres avec leurs cornes.

GOLD: OR

Gold is a yellow metal that is used to make jewels and coins.

This small gold ring belongs to Susan.
Ce petit anneau d'or appartient à Suzanne.

GOOD : BON(NE)

When something is good, it pleases you. Good is the opposite of bad.

Froggy's ice cream is really good.
La glace de Grenouillette est vraiment bonne.

GOOD-BYE : AU REVOIR

You say good-bye when you go away.

Teddy says good-bye to his friends.
Teddy dit au revoir à ses amis.

GORILLA : GORILLE

A gorilla is an animal from Africa with very long arms.

Gorillas love to swing from trees.
Les gorilles aiment se balancer aux arbres.

GRANDFATHER : GRAND-PÈRE

Your grandfather is your father's father or your mother's father.

Teddy's grandfather reads him a fairy tale.
Le grand-père de Teddy lui lit un conte de fées.

GRANDMOTHER : GRAND-MÈRE

Your grandmother is your father's mother or mother's mother.

Teddy's grandmother is knitting him a sweater.
La grand-mère de Teddy lui tricote un chandail.

GRANDPARENTS: GRANDS-PARENTS

Your grandparents are your father's parents or your mother's parents.

Teddy's grandparents live with him.
Les grands-parents de Teddy habitent chez lui.

GRAPES: RAISINS

Grapes are small green or purple fruits that grow in clusters on a vine.

This is a beautiful bunch of grapes.
C'est une magnifique grappe de raisins.

GRASS: HERBE

Grass is a green plant that grows in fields and lawns.

Ladybugs like to hide in the grass.
Les coccinelles aiment se cacher dans l'herbe.

GRASSHOPPER: CRIQUET

A grasshopper is an insect that has long hind legs and chirps.

Grasshoppers can hop long distances.
Les criquets peuvent sauter très loin.

GREEN: VERT

Green is the color of peas and of new grass in spring.

Marie is wearing her green skirt.
Marie porte sa jupe verte.

GUITAR: GUITARE

A guitar is a musical instrument that is played by plucking the strings with the fingers.

Elvis played the guitar.
Elvis a joué de la guitare.

HAIR: CHEVEUX

Hair is what grows on your head.

Barber Bruce has just combed Leo's hair.
Le coiffeur Bruce vient de peigner les cheveux de Léo.

HAMMER: MARTEAU

A hammer is a tool that is used to pound nails.

Mr. Rabbit is using a hammer to hang up some pictures.
Monsieur Lapin utilise un marteau pour accrocher des tableaux.

HAND: MAIN

Your hand is the part of your arm below the wrist.

Can you count the fingers on this hand?
Peux-tu compter les doigts de cette main?

HANDKERCHIEF: MOUCHOIR

You use a handkerchief to blow your nose or wipe your face.

Mousie's handkerchief is big indeed.
Le mouchoir de Souris est vraiment très grand.

HAPPY: HEUREUX

When you feel happy, you feel good inside.

Patty is happy when she can dance.
Pierrette est heureuse quand elle peut danser.

HAT: CHAPEAU

A hat keeps your head warm in winter and protects it from the sun in summer.

The gray hat is much too big for John.
Le chapeau gris est trop grand pour Jean.

HE: IL

He is a word for a boy or a man.

He is wearing a red T-shirt.
Il porte un t-shirt rouge.

HEAD: TÊTE

Your head is the part of your body above the neck.

Teddy's teacher is holding her head.
La maîtresse de Teddy soutient la tête.

HEAR: ENTENDRE

You hear sounds with your ears.

The elephant hears the sound of the drums.
L'éléphant entend le son des tambours.

HEART: COEUR

The heart is the part of your body that pumps blood. A heart is also a shape and the symbol of love.

Frank just drew a red heart.
François vient de dessiner un coeur rouge.

HEAVY: LOURD

Something heavy weighs a lot and is hard to lift.

The suitcase is too heavy for Gus.
La valise est trop lourde pour Gus.

HELICOPTER: HÉLICOPTÈRE

A helicopter is a machine that can fly straight up and down.

Captain Tiger rescues people with his red helicopter.

Le capitaine Tigre sauve des personnes avec son hélicoptère rouge.

HELMET: CASQUE

A helmet is a hard hat that protects your head.

Penguin always wears his helmet when he plays football.

Pingouin porte toujours son casque quand il joue au football américain.

HELP: AIDER

When you help people, you do something for them.

Teddy is helping his friend put away the toys.
Teddy aide son ami à ranger les jouets.

HI: BONJOUR

Hi is what we say to our friends when we see them.

Teddy always says hi to his uncle and to Joey.
Teddy dit toujours bonjour à son oncle et à Jacques.

HIPPOPOTAMUS : HIPPOPOTAME

A hippopotamus is a big African animal that spends a lot of time in rivers.

Hippos have gray skin.
Les hippopotames ont une peau grise.

HOLE : TROU

A hole is an empty, hollow place in something.

Cats know that mice hide in holes in the walls.
Les chats savent que les souris se cachent dans les trous du mur.

HOME : MAISON

Home is what we call the place where we live.

This nice little house is Teddy's home.
Cette jolie petite maison est la maison de Teddy.

HONEY : MIEL

Honey is a sweet, sticky food made by bees.

This jar is full of golden honey.
Ce pot est plein de miel doré.

HORSE: CHEVAL

A horse is an animal with a long mane and tail. Horses are lots of fun to ride.

Bert is a small, dappled-gray horse.
Beber est un petit cheval bai.

HOT: CHAUD

Hot means very, very warm. It's the way we feel in the summer.

It is hot in July.
Il fait chaud en juillet.

HOTEL: HÔTEL

A hotel is a building with many bedrooms where people stay when they are traveling.

Which city do you think this hotel is in?
Dans quelle ville croyez-vous que se trouve cet hôtel?

HOW MUCH?: COMBIEN?

We ask "How much?" when we want to know the price of something.

Mrs. Rabbit wants to know how much she has to pay.
Madame Lapin veut savoir combien elle doit payer.

HUNGRY (TO BE): FAIM (AVOIR)

You feel hungry when you haven't eaten in a long time.

Gus is very hungry and wants to eat the cheese.

Gus a très faim et veut manger le fromage.

I: JE

When you talk about yourself, you use the word *I*.

Quand tu parles de toi-même, dis je.

ICE: GLACE

Ice is frozen water.

There's lots of ice at the North Pole.

Il y en a beaucoup de glace au pôle Nord.

ICE CREAM: GLACE

Ice cream is a sweet food made from frozen cream and sugar.

Lou's favorite food is strawberry ice cream.

La nourriture favorite de Louis est la glace à la fraise.

IMPORTANT: IMPORTANT

When something is important, you should pay attention to it.

Vincent the Vulture always wants to seem very important.

Le vautour Vincent veut toujours paraître très important.

IN: DANS

We use the word *in* to show that something is located inside or within something else.

Henry is in his cell.
Henri est dans sa cellule.

INDIAN: INDIEN

An Indian is a native person of North or South America.

Teddy likes to dress up like a North American Indian.
Teddy aime s'habiller comme un indien d'Amérique.

ISLAND: ÎLE

An island is land that is completely surrounded by water.

The turtle is alone on a tropical island.
La tortue est seul dans une île tropicale.

ITALIAN: ITALIEN

An Italian is a person from Italy.
Un italien est originaire d'Italie.

JACKET: VESTE

A jacket is a short coat.

This nice blue jacket belongs to Teddy's father.
Cette jolie veste bleue appartient au père de Teddy.

JAM : CONFITURE

Jam is a food made from fruit and sugar that you spread on toast.

Piglet ate all the blackberry jam.
Cochonnet a mangé toute la confiture de mûres.

JANUARY : JANVIER

January is the first month of the year.

In January Andy likes to go ice skating.
En janvier André aime patiner.

JAPANESE : JAPONAIS

A Japanese person comes from Japan.
Un japonais est originaire de Japon.

JULY : JUILLET

July is the seventh month of the year.

In July it's nice to go swimming.
En juillet il est agréable d'aller nager.

JUMP : SAUTER

When you jump, you spring into the air.

Cricket can jump very far.
Criquet peut sauter très loin.

JUNE : JUIN

June is the sixth month of the year.

In June school is over for the summer.
En juin l'école est finie pour l'été.

KANGAROO : KANGOUROU

A kangaroo is an Australian animal with powerful hind legs. Kangaroos carry their babies in pouches.

Kangaroos can jump very far and very fast.
Les kangourous peuvent sauter très loin et très vite.

KEY : CLÉ

You use a key to unlock doors.

This is the key to Teddy's room.
C'est la clé de la chambre de Teddy.

KING : ROI

A king is the ruler of a kingdom or country.

Leo the Lion is the king of the jungle.
Le lion Léo est le roi de la jungle.

KISS: BAISER

A kiss is a touch with the lips to say *I love you*.

Baby Gorilla is happy when his mother gives him a kiss.
Le bébé gorille est content quand sa mère lui donne un baiser.

KITCHEN: CUISINE

The kitchen is a room where people cook meals.

Teddy gets a snack from the kitchen.
Teddy prend un casse-croûte de la cuisine.

LADDER: ÉCHELLE

A ladder is a tool that you climb to reach high places.

The firefighter uses the ladder to reach the window.
Le pompier utilise l'échelle pour atteindre la fenêtre.

LADYBUG: COCCINELLE

A ladybug is a very small beetle with bright red wings.

All ladybugs have black spots on their wings.
Toutes les coccinelles ont des taches noires sur les ailes.

LAKE: LAC

A lake is water that is surrounded by land.

The water in this lake is always clean and cool.
L'eau de ce lac est toujours propre et fraîche.

LAMP : LAMPE

You use a lamp to light your room when it gets dark.

This lamp is next to Teddy's bed.
Cette lampe est à côté du lit de Teddy.

LANGUAGE : LANGUE

Language is the words we speak, read, and write. Different countries have different languages.

Teddy learns a foreign language at school.
Teddy apprend une langue etrangère à l'école.

LATE : TARD

Late is the opposite of early.

Mr. Bear got to the station late and he missed his train.
Monsieur Ours est arrivé tard à la gare et il a manqué le train.

LAUGH : RIRE

To laugh means to make sounds when you think something is funny.

Tom the Tiger is laughing at a funny joke.
Le tigre Thomas rit d'une plaisanterie amusante.

LAWN: PELOUSE

A lawn is an area of grass around a house.

Piglet takes good care of his lawn.
Cochonnet soigne beaucoup sa pelouse.

LAZY: PARESSEUX

A lazy person doesn't want to work or do anything.

The lazy cat is sleeping in the sunshine.
Le chat paresseux dort au soleil.

LEAF: FEUILLE

A leaf is part of a plant.

This leaf just fell off the tree.
Cette feuille vient de tomber de l'arbre.

LEAVE: PARTIR

To leave means to go away.

Mr. Elephant is leaving by airplane.
Monsieur Éléphant part par avion.

LEFT: GAUCHE

Left is the opposite of right.

The policeman signals with his left arm.
Le policier fait un signe avec le bras gauche.

LEG: JAMBE

Your leg is the part of your body you stand and walk on.

Penguin went skiing and broke his right leg.
Pingouin est allé skier et s'est cassé la jambe droite.

LEMON: CITRON

A lemon is a sour, yellow fruit.

This bright yellow lemon is ripe.
Ce citron d'un jaune brillant est mûr.

LETTER: LETTRE

A letter is a message written on paper that you send to someone.

The mailman has a letter for Rachel.
Le facteur a une lettre pour Rachel.

LIE : MENTIR

When you don't tell the truth, you lie.

When Pinocchio lies, his nose gets longer.
Quand Pinocchio ment, son nez s'allonge.

LIGHT : LUMIÈRE

Light is energy that lets us see things.

Porcupine was surprised by a bright light.
Porc-épic a été surpris par une lumière brillante.

LIGHT : LÉGER (ÈRE)

Light is the opposite of heavy.

A feather is very light.
Une plume est très légère.

LIKE : AIMER

If you like something, it means it makes you happy.

This little mouse really likes cheese.
Cette petite souris aime beaucoup le fromage.

LION: LION

A lion is a huge cat that lives in Africa and Asia.

Leo the Lion looks ferocious.
Le lion Léo à l'air féroce.

LISTEN: ÉCOUTER

To listen means to try to hear carefully.

Tim the Gorilla listens to the radio.
Le gorille Tim écoute la radio.

LIVE: HABITER

To live means to dwell somewhere.

Teddy lives with his parents.
Teddy habite avec ses parents.

LONG: LONG

Long is the opposite of short.

Mrs. Hippopotamus's dress has a very long train.
La robe de Madame Hippopotame a une traîne très longue.

LOSE: PERDRE

When you lose something, you mislay it and cannot find it.

Piglet is losing all the seeds in his sack.
Cochonnet perd toutes les semences de son sac.

LUNCH: DÉJEUNER

Lunch is the second meal of the day.

Teddy takes his lunch to school in a paper bag.
Teddy emporte son déjeuner à l'école dans un sac en papier.

MAGICIAN: MAGICIEN

A magician uses magic to do all kinds of tricks.

Teddy the Magician just made an ice-cream cone appear.
Le magicien Teddy vient de faire apparaître un cornet de glace.

MAILMAN: FACTEUR

The mailman delivers letters and packages to your house.

Toby the Turtle is the fastest mailman in town.
La tortue Tobie est le facteur le plus rapide de la ville.

MAN: HOMME

A man is an adult male person.

My dad is a very elegant man.
Mon père est un homme très élégant.

MARCH: MARS

March is the third month of the year.

March is always very windy.
En mars il y a toujours beaucoup de vent.

MATCH: MATCH

A match is a game between two players or two teams.

Joey's team won the basketball match.
L'équipe de Jacques a gagné le match de basket-ball.

MATH: MATHÉMATIQUES

Math is the study of numbers, shapes, and measurements.

Teddy is not very good at math.
Teddy n'est pas très fort en mathématiques.

MAY: MAI

May is the fifth month of the year.

Mother's Day is celebrated in May.
La fête des mères se célèbre en mai.

ME: ME, MOI

Me is a word you use when you speak about yourself.

Anne wrote a letter to me.
Anne m'a écrit une lettre.

MEAT: VIANDE

Meat is the part of an animal we use as food.

A pork chop is one kind of meat.
Une côtelette de porc est un type de viande.

MEDICINE: MÉDICAMENT

Medicine is what we take when we're ill to help us get well.

Oscar the Ostrich doesn't want to take his medicine.
L'autruche Oscar ne veut pas prendre son médicament.

MESS: DÉSORDRE

Something is a mess when things are not in the right place.

Look at the mess on this desk!
Regarde ce désordre sur ce bureau!

MIDNIGHT: MINUIT

Midnight is twelve o'clock at night.

The tower clock has just struck midnight.
L'horloge de la tour vient de sonner minuit.

MILK: LAIT

Milk is a white liquid that we drink. It usually comes from cows.

Someone left some milk in the glass.
Quelqu'un a laissé un peu de lait dans le verre.

MIRROR: MIROIR

A mirror is a piece of polished glass that reflects your image.

Leo the Lion admires his new hairdo in the mirror.
Le lion Léo admire sa nouvelle coiffure dans le miroir.

MISS: MADEMOISELLE

We call an unmarried girl or young woman *miss*.

Miss Jackson is our teacher.
Mademoiselle Jackson est notre maîtresse.

MOMMY: MAMAN

Small children call their mothers *Mommy*.

Teddy's mommy loves him very much.
La maman de Teddy l'aime beaucoup.

MONDAY: LUNDI

Monday is the very first day of the week.

Every Monday Teddy goes swimming.
Tous les lundis Teddy va nager.

MONEY: ARGENT

Money is used to buy things.

Mr. Greedy is always counting
his money.
*Monsieur Rapace compte toujours
son argent.*

MONKEY: SINGE

A monkey is a furry animal, with very long
arms and legs.

Monkeys love to eat bananas.
Les singes aiment manger des bananes.

MONTH: MOIS

There are twelve months in one year.

The calendar shows what month it is.
Le calendrier montre le mois courant.

MOON: LUNE

The moon revolves around the earth in the
sky.

Wolfgang the Wolf howls at the moon.
Le loup Wolfgang hurle à la lune.

MORNING: MATIN

Morning is the part of the day before noon.

Mr. Leopard gets up early
in the morning.
*Monsieur Léopard se lève
tôt le matin.*

MOSQUITO: MOUSTIQUE

A mosquito is a small, flying insect.

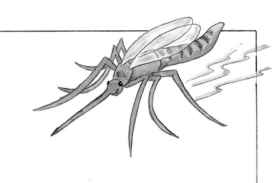

Zip is the fastest mosquito I know.
Zip est le moustique le plus rapide que je connaisse.

MOTHER: MÈRE

A mother is a woman with one or more children.

Teddy loves his mother.
Teddy aime sa mère.

MOTORCYCLE: MOTOCYCLETTE

A motorcycle looks like a bicycle with a motor.

Teddy wears a helmet when he rides his motorcycle.
Teddy porte un casque quand il va en motocyclette.

MOUNTAIN: MONTAGNE

A mountain is a high peak of land.

This high mountain has snow on top.
Cette haute montagne a de la neige au sommet.

MOUSE: SOURIS

A mouse is a very small animal with a long tail.

The mouse ran up the clock.
La souris est montée à l'horloge.

MOUTH : BOUCHE

Your mouth is used to eat and speak, and kiss with.

Crocodiles have huge mouths.
Les crocodiles ont des bouches énormes.

MOVIE : CINÉMA

A movie is a film made of pictures that move.

Teddy buys a ticket for the movie.
Teddy achète un billet pour le cinéma.

MR. : MONSIEUR

We call men *Mr.*

Mr. Rabbit reads the newspaper.
Monsieur Lapin lit le journal.

MRS. : MADAME

We call a married woman *Mrs.*

Mrs. Bear is Teddy's mother.
Madame Ours est la mère de Teddy.

MUSIC : MUSIQUE

Music is the sound made by the voice or by instruments.

This small band plays great music.
Ce petit orchestre joue une musique superbe.

NAIL: CLOU

A nail is a thin piece of metal with a pointed tip that is used to fasten things.

Pete hits the nail with the hammer.
Pierre frappe le clou avec le marteau.

NAME: NOM

A name is a word that you call something by.

Marie's name is printed on her shirt.
Le nom de Marie est imprimé sur sa chemise.

NECK: COU

Your neck connects your head to the rest of your body.

Giraffes have very long necks.
Les girafes ont des cous très longs.

NECKLACE: COLLIER

A necklace is a chain or a string of beads that is worn around the neck.

This necklace is made of beautiful green stones.
Ce collier est fait de magnifiques pierres vertes.

NEEDLE : AIGUILLE

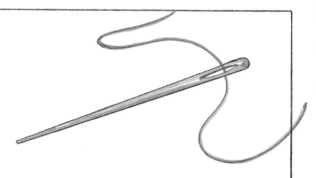

A needle is a slender piece of steel that is used to sew.

Here's a needle with blue thread.
Voici une aiguille et du fil bleu.

NEW : NEUF (NEUVE)

Something new has never been used or worn before.

Julia is very proud of her new hat.
Julie est très fière de son chapeau neuf.

NEWSPAPER : JOURNAL

You read the newspaper to find out what is going on in the world.

Mr. Rabbit can never read his newspaper in peace.
Monsieur Lapin ne peut jamais lire son journal en paix.

NIGHT : NUIT

Night is the part of the day when it is dark outside.

The moon and stars shine at night.
La lune et les étoiles brillent la nuit.

NINE: NEUF

Nine is the number after eight and before ten.

Here are nine strawberries in a row.
Voici neuf fraises rouges côte à côte.

NO: NON, NE, N'

No is the opposite of yes.

The sign says that no hunting is allowed.
La pancarte dit qu'il n'est pas permis de chasser.

NOISE: BRUIT

A noise is a sound, usually a loud one.

The band is making a lot of noise.
L'orchestre fait beaucoup de bruit.

NOON: MIDI

Noon is twelve o'clock in the day.

It's exactly noon on the tower clock.
Il est exactement midi à l'horloge de la tour.

NOSE : NEZ

Your nose is in the center of your face.

Pinocchio's nose is now very long.
Le nez de Pinocchio est très long maintenant.

NOVEMBER : NOVEMBRE

November is the eleventh month of the year.

In November all the leaves fall from the trees.
En novembre toutes les feuilles tombent des arbres.

NURSE : INFIRMIÈRE

A nurse is a person who looks after sick people.

Teddy's mother is a very good nurse.
La mère de Teddy est une très bonne infirmière.

OCTOBER : OCTOBRE

October is the tenth month of the year.

Halloween is celebrated on October 31.
Halloween se célèbre le 31 octobre.

OFFICE : BUREAU

An office is a place where people work.

This is the office where Teddy's father works.
C'est le bureau où travaille le père de Teddy.

OLD : VIEUX (VIEILLE)

Old things have been used for a long time. Old people have lived many years.

This is a very old shoe.
Cette chaussure est très vieille.

ONE : UN

One is a number more than zero and less than two.

Here is one big, green watermelon.
Voici une grosse pastèque verte.

ONE HUNDRED : CENT

One hundred is ten times ten.

There are one hundred cherries in this basket.
Il y a cent cerises dans ce panier.

ONE THOUSAND: MILLE

One thousand is ten times one hundred.

Now there are one thousand cherries in this basket.

Maintenant il y a mille cerises dans ce panier.

ONION: OIGNON

An onion is an edible bulb that has a very strong smell and taste.

Teddy's mother cries when she cuts onions.

La mère de Teddy pleure quand elle coupe des oignons.

OPEN: OUVRIR

To open is the opposite of to close or to shut.

The front door is open.

La porte d'entrée est ouverte.

ORANGE: ORANGE

An orange is a juicy fruit with a thick rind.

We have to peel oranges before we eat them.

Nous devons peler les oranges avant de les manger.

OSTRICH: AUTRUCHE

An ostrich is a very large bird that lives in Africa.

Ostriches can't fly, but they can run very fast.
Les autruches ne peuvent pas voler, mais ils peuvent courir très vite.

OUT: HORS

Out is the opposite of in.

Henry is now out of jail.
Henri est maintenant hors de prison.

PAGE: PAGE

A page is one side of a piece of paper in a book, magazine, or newspaper.

This page in Teddy's book has two big pictures.
Cette page du livre de Teddy a deux grandes images.

PAINTER: PEINTRE

A painter is a person who paints.

Teddy would like to be a famous painter.
Teddy aimerait être un peintre fameux.

PAJAMAS: PYJAMA

Pajamas are a shirt and pants that we wear when we go to bed.

Rhino and his wife are sharing a pair of pajamas.
Rhino et sa femme se sont partagé un pyjama.

PANDA: PANDA

A panda is an animal that lives in Asia and looks like a big black-and-white bear.

Pandas are a protected species.
Les pandas sont une espèce protégée.

PANTS: PANTALON

Pants are clothes with two long legs.

These pants are too big for Arthur.
Ce pantalon est trop grand pour Arthur.

PAPER: PAPIER

Paper is a material made from trees that you can write on.

The present is wrapped in pretty paper.
Le cadeau est emballé dans du joli papier.

76

PARACHUTE: PARACHUTE

A parachute is used to drop people or things safely from an airplane.

Christopher's parachute opened right after he jumped out of the plane.
Le parachute de Christophe est ouvert juste après qu'il a sauté de l'avion.

PARENT: PARENT

Your father and your mother are your parents.

Teddy's parents play with their children.
Les parents de Teddy jouen avec leurs enfants.

PARK: PARC

A park is a public garden with trees and grass and places where you can play.

This park has a slide, a swing, a sand box, and a seesaw.
Ce parc a un tobogan, une balançoire, un bac de sable, et une bascule.

PARROT: PERROQUET

A parrot is a tropical bird with brightly colored feathers.

This parrot can speak.
Ce perroquet peut parler.

PEA: PETIT POIS

A pea is a small, round, green vegetable.

This pod has five peas in it.
Il y a cinq petits pois dans cette gousse.

PEACH: PÊCHE

A peach is a sweet, juicy fruit with a fuzzy peel.

This peach is now perfectly ripe.
Cette pêche est maintenant tout à fait mûre.

PEAR: POIRE

A pear is a green, sometimes yellow, fruit.

Pears are wider at the bottom than at the top.
Les poires sont plus larges à la base qu'au sommet.

PEN: STYLO

A pen is filled with ink and is used to write.

This is a special ballpoint pen.
C'est un stylo à bille spécial.

PENCIL: CRAYON

You use a pencil to write or draw.

We can color the sea or the sky with this pencil.
Nous pouvons colorier la mer ou le ciel avec ce crayon.

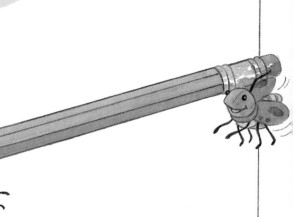

PENGUIN : PINGOUIN

A penguin is a short-legged bird that lives in Antarctica and can't fly.

Penguins look like they're wearing tuxedos.
Les pingouins semblent porter un frac.

PHOTOGRAPH : PHOTOGRAPHIE

We take a photograph with a camera.

Cricket is taking a photograph of seven ladybugs.
Criquet fait une photographie de sept coccinelles.

PICTURE : TABLEAU

A picture is a drawing or painting.

In this picture Piglet has a black eye.
Sur ce tableau Cochonnet a un oeil au beurre noir.

PIG : COCHON

A pig is a farm animal with a snout and a short, curly tail.

The pig is a domestic animal.
Le cochon est un animal domestique.

PINEAPPLE: ANANAS

A pineapple is a yellowish fruit that grows in the tropics and has a thick, rough peel.

This pineapple was grown in Hawaii.
Cet ananas a poussé à Hawaii.

PINK: ROSE

Pink is a color made by mixing red with white.

Roses, flamingos, and baby pigs are pink.
Les roses, les flamants, et les petits cochons sont roses.

PLAY: JOUER

To play means to do something for fun.

Teddy plays checkers with his friend.
Teddy joue aux échecs avec son ami.

PLAY: JOUER

To play means to perform music on an instrument.

Piglet is learning to play the trombone.
Cochonnet apprend à jouer du trombone.

PLEASE: S'IL VOUS (TE) PLAÎT

Please is a word you say when you ask for something politely.

Please buy me an ice cream cone.
Achète-moi un cornet de glace, s'il te plaît.

POCKET: POCHE

A pocket is a place that holds things.

Tim's pockets are empty.
Les poches de Tim sont vides.

POINT: INDIQUER

To point means to use your finger to show something.

Eddie is pointing with both his fingers and his toes.
Édouard indique avec les mains et les pieds.

POLICEMAN: POLICIER

A policeman helps keep public order and safety.

Pat is a very serious but very kind policeman.
Pat est un policier très sérieux mais très gentil.

POLITE: POLI

When you are polite, you behave in a courteous and considerate manner.

Joey is always very polite and kind.
Jacques est toujours très poli et très aimable.

PORT: PORT

A port is a place where ships dock.

This is a very important and active port.
C'est un port très important et très actif.

POTATO: POMME DE TERRE

A potato is a vegetable that grows underground.

We eat baked potatoes for dinner.
Nous mangeons des pommes de terre au four pour dîner.

PRESENT: CADEAU

A present is a gift you give on a special occasion.

Mrs. Rabbit bought many presents for Charlie.
Madame Lapin a acheté beaucoup de cadeaux pour Charles.

PRIZE : PRIX

People get a prize when they win a contest or a competition.

Phil's team won first prize.
L'équipe de Philippe a gagné le premier prix.

PULL : TIRER

You pull when you want to move something toward you.

If they pull too hard, they'll tear the scarf.
S'ils tirent trop fort, ils déchireront le foulard.

PUMPKIN : CITROUILLE

A pumpkin is a big, orange fruit that grows on a vine.

Teddy made a jack-o'-lantern from a pumpkin.
Teddy a fabriqué une lanterne avec une citrouille.

PURPLE : POURPRE

Purple is a color made by mixing red with blue.

Eggplants, plums, and violets are purple.
Les aubergines, les prunes, et les violettes sont pourpres.

PUSH: POUSSER

Push is the opposite of pull. You push when you want to move something away from you.

Rhino is so clumsy that he pushes everybody.
Rhino est si maladroit qu'il pousse tout le monde.

QUEEN: REINE

A queen is the wife of a king or the head of a kingdom in her own right.

Queen Leona is the wife of King Leo.
La reine Léonie est la femme du roi Léo.

QUESTION: QUESTION

We ask a question when we don't know or aren't sure of something.

Teddy asks his teacher a question.
Teddy pose une question à sa maîtresse.

RABBIT: LAPIN

A rabbit is a small, furry animal with a soft tail.

Rabbits have long, pointed ears, and short, round tails.
Les lapins ont de longues oreilles pointues et une queue ronde et courte.

RADIO: RADIO

A radio is a machine that plays music and news broadcasts.

Tim has a small portable radio.
Tim a une petite radio portative.

RAIN: PLUIE

Rain is water that falls from the clouds.

When there's rain, we stay indoors.
Quand la pluie tombe, nous restons à la maison.

RAINBOW: ARC-EN-CIEL

A rainbow is colors that appear in the sky after it rains.

There's a pot of gold at the end of the rainbow.
Il y a un vase d'or au bout de l'arc-en-ciel.

RAINCOAT: IMPERMÉABLE

A raincoat is a coat you wear to keep dry in the rain.

Joey has a yellow raincoat.
Jacques a un imperméable jaune.

READ: LIRE

When you know how to read, you can understand written words.

Mr. Rabbit reads the newspaper every day.
Monsieur Lapin lit le journal tous les jours.

RED: ROUGE

Red is the color of fire engines and ketchup.

Hearts and strawberries are red.
Les coeurs et les fraises sont rouges.

REFRIGERATOR: RÉFRIGÉRATEUR

A refrigerator is a machine that keeps food cold.

This refrigrator is full of good things.
Ce réfrigérateur est plein de bonnes choses.

RESTAURANT: RESTAURANT

A restaurant is a place to eat away from home.

This is a very famous and very good restaurant.
C'est un restaurant très bon et très fameux.

RHINOCEROS: RHINOCÉROS

A rhinoceros is a large African animal with one or two horns on its snout.

The rhinoceros has short legs, but it can run very fast.
Le rhinocéros a des pattes courtes, mais il peut courir très vite.

RICE: RIZ

Rice is a white grain that is eaten for food.

Teddy eats rice with chopsticks.
Teddy mange le riz avec des baguettes.

RICH: RICHE

Rich is the opposite of poor. Rich people have lots of money.

Mr. Greedy is very, very rich.
Monsieur Rapace est très, très riche.

RIGHT: DROIT

Right is the opposite of left.

The policeman signals with his right arm.
Le policier fait un signal avec son bras droit.

RING: BAGUE

A ring is a piece of jewelry that you wear on your finger.

This ring has a very pretty stone.
Cette bague a une très jolie pierre.

RIVER: FLEUVE

A river is water that flows toward the sea or a lake.

Hippo is rowing down the river.
Hippo rame sur le fleuve.

ROAD: ROUTE

A road is a wide path that cars travel on.

Do you know where this long road leads to?
Sais-tu où va cette route si longue?

ROBOT: ROBOT

A robot is a machine that can do some things that people do.

This robot can stand on its head.
Ce robot peut se tenir sur la tête.

ROOF : TOIT

A roof is the top part of a building.

This house has a red, slanted roof.
Cette maison a un toit rouge et incliné.

RUN : COURIR

Run means to move with your legs as fast as you can.

Teddy and his friend run in a race.
Teddy et ses amis font la course.

SAIL : VOILE

A sail is a large piece of cloth that catches the wind to make a boat move forward.

Jumbo's boat has a small sail.
La barque de Jumbo a une petite voile.

SALAD : SALADE

A salad is a cold food made with vegetables, fruits, or meat.

This is a lettuce and tomato salad.
C'est une salade de laitue et de tomates.

SAND : SABLE
Sand is made of tiny pieces of rock.

In the desert there are tons and tons of sand.
Dans le désert il y a des milliers de tonnes de sable.

SANTA CLAUS : PÈRE NOËL
Santa Claus brings children presents on Christmas Eve.

Santa Claus has a trumpet for Tim.
Le père Noël a une trompette pour Tim.

SATURDAY : SAMEDI
Saturday is the sixth day of the week.

Teddy and his sister watch cartoons on Saturday.
Teddy et sa soeur regardent les dessins animés le samedi.

SAUSAGE : SAUCISSE
A sausage is made of ground meat and spices.

Sausages are attached to one another with a string.
Les saucisses sont attachées par une cordelette.

SCALE: BALANCE

A scale is a machine used to weigh things.

Hippo broke the scale.
Hippo a cassé la balance.

SCHOOL: ÉCOLE

School is a place where people learn things from teachers.

Children go to school every morning.
Les enfants vont à l'école tous les matins.

SCISSORS: CISEAUX

Scissors are a tool used for cutting.

Teddy cuts paper with scissors.
Teddy coupe du papier avec les ciseaux.

SEA: MER

The sea is made of salt water.

Beaver takes his canoe to sea every summer.
Castor emmène son canot à la mer chaque été.

SEAL: PHOQUE

A seal is an animal that swims in the ocean and has smooth fur.

Sam the Seal is sleeping on a warm rock.
Le phoque Sam dort sur un rocher tiède.

SEASON: SAISON

Spring, summer, fall, and winter are the four seasons.

Le printemps, l'été, l'automne, et l'hiver sont les quatre saisons.

SEE: VOIR

To see means to look at something with your eyes.

Cats can see in the dark.
Les chats peuvent voir dans l'obscurité.

SEPTEMBER: SEPTEMBRE

September is the ninth month of the year.

In September Teddy goes back to school.
En septembre Teddy retourne à l'école.

SEVEN: SEPT

Seven is the number after six and before eight.

Here are seven plums all in a row.
Voici sept prunes violettes côte à côte.

SHARK: REQUIN

A shark lives in the sea and has very sharp teeth.

Sharks are ferocious-looking animals.
Les requins sont des animaux à l'air féroce.

SHE: ELLE

She is a word for a girl or a woman.
Elle se dit pour une fille ou une femme.

SHEEP: MOUTON

A sheep is an animal with curly hair that we use for wool.

Mrs. Sheep is knitting a sweater for her lamb.
Madame Mouton tricote un chandail pour son agneau.

SHERIFF: SHÉRIF

A sheriff helped keep law and order in the Wild West.

Teddy's grandfather was a sheriff in Arizona.
Le grand-père de Teddy était shérif en Arizona.

SHIP: BATEAU

A ship is a big boat that can sail the seven seas.

A brave captain stays on board when his ship sinks.
Un capitaine courageux reste à bord quand son bateau coule.

SHIRT: CHEMISE

A shirt is a piece of clothing that covers the top part of your body.

Michael's white shirt isn't very white!
La chemise blanche de Michel n'est pas très blanche!

SHOE: CHAUSSURE

Shoes protect our feet when we walk.

This is a comfortable running shoe.
Cette chaussure est pratique pour courir.

SHOP: MAGASIN

A shop is a place where you can buy things.

This shop has all kinds of toys.
Ce magasin a toutes sortes de jouets.

SHORT: COURT

Short is the opposite of long.

Mrs. Hippopotamus's dress is too short.
La robe de Madame Hippopotame est trop courte.

SHOWER: DOUCHE

A shower is a spray of water to wash in.

Sammy's shower is a red watering can.
La douche de Sammy est un arrosoir rouge.

SICK: MALADE

When you are sick, you do not feel well.

Doggy is sick, and so he stays in bed.
Doggy est malade, donc il reste au lit.

SINGER: CHANTEUR

A singer is a person who sings songs.

Annie is a great singer.
Annie est une grande chanteuse.

SISTER: SOEUR

Your sister is a girl who has the same father and mother as you do.

Rachel is Theo's little sister.
Rachel est la petite soeur de Théo.

SIT DOWN: S'ASSEOIR

To sit down means to rest your bottom on something.

Mr. Rabbit sits down in front of the television.
Monsieur Lapin s'assied devant la télévision.

SIX: SIX

Six is the number after five and before seven.

Here are six green pears all in a row.
Voici six poires vertes côte à côte.

SKI: SKIER

To ski means to move over snow on skis.

Penguin loves to ski in the winter.
Pingouin aime faire du ski en hiver.

SKIRT: JUPE

A skirt is a piece of clothing that women and girls wear.

This is Linda's favorite skirt.
C'est la jupe préférée de Linda.

SKY: CIEL

The sky is above you when you are outdoors.

There is a rainbow in the sky.
Il y a un arc-en-ciel dans le ciel.

SKYSCRAPER: GRATTE-CIEL

A skyscraper is a very tall building.

The Empire State Building is a famous skyscraper.
L'Empire State Building est un gratte-ciel fameux.

SLEEP: DORMIR

To sleep is to rest with your eyes closed.

Piglet is sleeping under a tree.
Cochonnet dort sous un arbre.

SLEIGH: TRAÎNEAU

A sleigh is used to move about on snow or ice.

Santa Claus has a sleigh at the North Pole.
Père Noël a un traîneau au pôle Nord.

SLOW: LENT

Slow is the opposite of fast.

Snails are very slow.
Les escargots sont très lents.

SNAKE: SERPENT

A snake is a long, thin reptile with no legs.

Snakes don't walk, they crawl.
Les serpents ne marchent pas, ils rampent.

SNOW: NEIGE

Snow is rain that freezes.

Piglet and Theo are playing in the snow.
Cochonnet et Théo jouent dans la neige.

SO LONG: SALUT

So long is a friendly way of saying good-bye.

Teddy says "So long" to his friend.
Teddy dit "Salut" à son ami.

SOAP: SAVON

Soap is used to wash and clean things.

This bar of soap is pink.
Ce savon est rose.

SOCCER: FOOTBALL

Soccer is a game played with a round ball between two teams on a field.

Rhino plays soccer too roughly.
Rhino joue au football trop violemment.

SOCK: CHAUSSETTE

A sock is a soft cover for your foot.

Dino has only one red sock on.
Dino a mis seulement une chaussette rouge.

SOFA: CANAPÉ

A sofa is a soft seat for two or more people.

Three people can sit on this comfortable sofa.
Trois personnes peuvent s'asseoir sur ce canapé.

SON: FILS

A son is the male child of a mother and a father.

Teddy's parents have two sons.
Les parents de Teddy ont deux fils.

SORRY: PARDON

We say "Sorry" when we want to apologize.

Piglet says "I'm sorry" when he steps on someone's foot.
Cochonnet dit "Pardon" quand il marche sur les pieds de quelqu'un.

SOUP: SOUPE

Soup is a liquid that you eat with a spoon.

The soup is delicious.
La soupe est délicieuse.

SPACESHIP: VAISSEAU SPATIAL

A spaceship carries astronauts to outer space.

This spaceship is traveling to Mars.
Ce vaisseau spatial fait route vers Mars.

SPANIARD: ESPAGNOL

A Spaniard is a native of Spain.
Un espagnol est originaire d'Espagne.

SPIDER: ARAIGNÉE

A spider is a small animal with eight legs.

Spiders weave very fine cobwebs.
Les araignées tissent des toiles très fines.

SPINACH: ÉPINARD

Spinach is a vegetable with dark green leaves.

Mrs. Rabbit buys spinach for her children.
Madame Lapin achète des épinards pour ses enfants.

SPORT: SPORT

A sport is a game that we play for fun and for exercise.

Pete the Octopus plays all kinds of sports.
La pieuvre Pierre pratique tous les sports.

SPRING: PRINTEMPS

Spring is the season when the days get warm and the trees get new leaves.

In spring Ella plants beans in her garden.
Au printemps Ella plante des haricots dans son jardin.

SQUIRREL: ÉCUREUIL

A squirrel is a small, furry animal that eats nuts.

Squirrels have long, bushy tails.
Les écureuils ont des queues longues et épaisses.

STAMP: TIMBRE

A stamp is a small piece of paper you put on a letter that has to be mailed.

This stamp is from Leo's Jungle Kingdom.
Ce timbre est du Royaume de la Jungle de Léo.

STAR: ÉTOILE

A star is a small, bright light in the night sky.

There are fifty stars on the American flag.
Il y a cinquante étoiles sur le drapeau américain.

STEAK: BIFTECK

A steak is a piece of beef.

This is a broiled steak.
C'est un bifteck grillé.

STOP: S'ARRETER

Stop is the opposite of go.

The policeman ordered Rhino to stop.
Le policier a ordonné à Rhino de s'arrêter.

STRAWBERRY: FRAISE

A strawberry is a small, red, juicy fruit.

Strawberries are especially good with cream.
Les fraises sont particulièrement bonnes avec de la crème.

STRONG: FORT

If you are strong, you are physically powerful.

Elephants are very strong.
Les éléphants sont très forts.

STUDENT: ÉTUDIANT

A student is a person who goes to school.
Un étudiant est une personne qui va à l'école.

STUDY: ÉTUDIER

When you study, you try hard to learn.

Arthur studies hard for his exam.
Arthur étudie beaucoup pour son examen.

SUBMARINE: SOUS-MARIN

A submarine is a ship that travels underwater.

This green submarine travels to the bottom of the sea.
Ce sous-marin vert va au fond de la mer.

SUIT : COMPLET

A suit is made up of a jacket and a pair of pants or a skirt.

This suit has a blue jacket and gray pants.
Ce complet se compose d'une veste bleue et d'un pantalon gris.

SUITCASE : VALISE

We pack our clothes in a suitcase when we travel.

Teddy packed his suitcase yesterday.
Teddy a fait sa valise hier.

SUMMER : ÉTÉ

Summer is the hottest season of the year.

In summer we gather the crops.
En été nous faisons la moisson.

SUN : SOLEIL

The sun is a star that gives us light and heat.

On a clear day, the sun shines brightly.
Quand il fait beau, le soleil brille.

SUNDAY: DIMANCHE

Sunday is the seventh day of the week.

Teddy's family goes to church on Sundays.
La famille de Teddy va à l'église le dimanche.

SURPRISE: SURPRISE

A surprise is something unexpected.

Jane's present was a complete surprise.
Le cadeau de Jeanne était une vraie surprise.

SWEATER: CHANDAIL

A sweater is a warm piece of clothing that you wear on the top part of your body.

Andy and his friend are sharing a huge sweater.
André et son ami se partagent un chandail énorme.

SWIM: NAGER

To swim means to move in the water.

Turtles, frogs, and fish love to swim.
Les tortues, les grenouilles, et les poissons aiment nager.

TABLE : TABLE

A table is a piece of furniture with four legs and a flat top.

This table is big but not very high.
Cette table est grande mais n'est pas très haute.

TAIL : QUEUE

A tail is the part of an animal's body at the end of its back.

Felix takes good care of his lovely tail.
Felix prend soin de sa belle queue.

TAKE : PRENDRE

To take means to bring or to carry or to get hold of something.

The big cat takes a book from the shelf.
Le grand chat prend un livre sur l'étagère.

TALL : GRAND

Tall is the opposite of short.

Giraffes are very tall animals.
Les girafes sont des animaux très grands.

TAXI: TAXI

A taxi is a car that carries passengers for a fare.

This is a little yellow taxi.
Voici un petit taxi jaune.

TEACHER: MAÎTRESSE

A teacher is a person who helps people learn.

Mrs. Bear is a very good teacher.
Madame Ours est une très bonne maîtresse.

TELEPHONE: TÉLÉPHONE

We use a telephone when we want to talk to someone who is far away.

Who forgot to hang up the telephone?
Qui a oublié de raccrocher le téléphone?

TELEVISION: TÉLÉVISION

A television shows pictures with sound in our homes.

There are lots of cartoons on television.
Il y a beaucoup de dessins animés à la télévision.

TEN: DIX

Ten is the number after nine and before eleven.

Here are ten small red cherries all in a row.
Voici dix petites cerises rouges côte à côte.

TENNIS COURT: COURT DE TENNIS

A tennis court is where you play tennis.

Tennis players have to be very fast on the tennis court.
Les joueurs de tennis doivent être très rapides sur le court de tennis.

THANK YOU: MERCI

We say "Thank you" when someone does something for us.

Arthur the Crocodile says "Thank you" with a bow.
Le crocodile Arthur fait la révérence en disant merci.

THEATER: THÉÂTRE

A theater is a place where plays and concerts are performed.

Hippo sings opera in a small theater.
Hippo chante l'opéra dans un petit théâtre.

THIN: MINCE

Thin is the opposite of fat or thick.

Sammy the Snake is very, very thin.
Le serpent Sammy est très, très mince.

THINK: PENSER

To think means to use your mind.

Teddy's father is thinking about his vacation.
Le père de Teddy pense à ses vacances.

THIRSTY: SOIF (AVOIR)

When you are thirsty, you want something to drink.

You can get very thirsty in the desert.
Vous pouvez avoir très soif dans le désert.

THREE: TROIS

Three is the number after two and before four.

Here are three yellow bananas all in a row.
Voici trois bananes jaunes côte à côte.

THURSDAY: JEUDI

Thursday is the fourth day of the week.

On Thursday Annie takes violin lessons.
Le jeudi Annie prend des cours de violon.

TIE: CRAVATE

A tie is a piece of men's clothing that is worn with a shirt and a jacket.

Teddy's tie is much too long.
La cravate de Teddy est trop longue.

TIGER: TIGRE

Tigers are big, striped cats that live in Asia.

You can recognize a tiger by its black stripes.
Tu peux reconnaître un tigre à ses rayures noires.

TIRED: FATIGUÉ

When you are tired, you need to sleep or rest.

Andy is tired because he has walked all day.
André est fatigué parce qu'il a marché toute la journée.

TOMATO: TOMATE

A tomato is a red fruit that we use in salads, sauces, and sandwiches.

Ripe tomatoes are bright red.
Les tomates mûres sont d'un rouge intense.

TONGUE: LANGUE

Your tongue is part of your mouth, and it helps you to speak, to eat, and to taste your food.

Rene wants to see his tongue.
René veut voir sa langue.

TOOTH: DENT

A tooth is one of the hard, white parts in your mouth.

Hippo has lost a tooth.
Hippo a perdu une dent.

TOOTHPASTE: DENTIFRICE

We use toothpaste to help clean our teeth.

Toothpaste comes in a tube.
Le dentifrice est en tube.

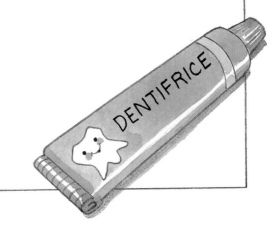

TOWEL : SERVIETTE

A towel is a piece of cloth used to dry or wipe things.

Piglet is drying himself with a towel.
Cochonnet s'essuie avec une serviette.

TOWN : VILLE

A town is a small city.

Teddy goes to school in town.
Teddy va à l'école en ville.

TOY : JOUET

A toy is something children play with.

Dolls, blocks, and balls are all toys.
Les poupées, les blocs, et les balles sont tous des jouets.

TRAFFIC LIGHT : FEU

A traffic light tells cars and people when to go and when to stop.

Teddy stops because the traffic light is red.
Teddy s'arrête parce que le feu est rouge.

TRAIN : TRAIN

A train moves on rails and carries people and things from one place to another.

James and his train ran through the fence.
Jacques et son train ont traversé la clôture.

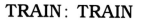

TRAVEL: VOYAGER

To travel is to go from one place to another.

Tim travels far in his small, red car.
Tim voyage loin dans sa petite auto rouge.

TREASURE: TRÉSOR

A treasure is something of great value.

Pirates are happy when they find a treasure.
Les pirates sont contents quand ils trouvent un trésor.

TREE: ARBRE

A tree is a plant with a trunk, branches, and leaves or needles.

Firs and pines are trees that are always green, even in winter.
Les sapins et les pins sont des arbres toujours verts, même en hiver.

TRUCK: CAMION

A truck is a vehicle that carries big, heavy things.

Ralph drives a big, green truck.
Ralph conduit un grand camion vert.

TRUMPET: TROMPETTE

A trumpet is a wind instrument made of brass.

Criquet likes to hide in Rhino's trumpet.
Criquet aime se cacher dans la trompette de Rhino.

TUESDAY: MARDI

Tuesday is the second day of the week.

On Tuesday Annie studies English in class.
Le mardi Annie étudie l'anglais en classe.

TUMMY: VENTRE

Your tummy is the part of your body between the chest and hips.

Hippo is proud of his tummy.
Hippo est fier de son ventre.

TURKEY: DINDE

A turkey is a big bird that is raised for food.

We eat turkey for Thanksgiving dinner.
Nous mangeons de la dinde pour Thanksgiving.

TURTLE: TORTUE

A turtle is an animal with a hard shell.

Turtles are never in a hurry.
Les tortues ne sont jamais pressées.

TWINS: JUMEAUX

Twins are two children who are born at the same time to the same mother.

Some twins are identical.
Les jumeaux sont quelquefois identiques.

TWO: DEUX

Two is the number after one and before three.

Here are two big, juicy pineapples.
Voici deux gros ananas juteux.

TYPEWRITER: MACHINE À ÉCRIRE

A typewriter is a machine with a keyboard that we use to write with.

This is Teddy's father's typewriter.
C'est la machine à écrire du père de Teddy.

T-SHIRT: T-SHIRT
A T-shirt has short sleeves and no collar.

Andy's favorite T-shirt is red.
Le T-shirt préféré d'André est rouge.

UGLY: LAID
Ugly is the opposite of beautiful.

Bruno tries to make himself ugly.
Bruno essaye de se rendre laid.

UMBRELLA: PARAPLUIE
An umbrella is used to protect us from the rain.

Froggy closes his umbrella because it has stopped raining.
Grenouillette ferme son parapluie parce qu'il a cessé de pleuvoir.

UNCLE: ONCLE
An uncle is your father's or your mother's brother.
Un oncle est le frère de ton père ou de ta mère.

UNITED STATES: ÉTATS-UNIS
The United States is a big country. The capital is Washington, D.C.
Les États-Unis sont un grand pays. La capitale est Washington, D.C.

VACATION: VACANCES

A vacation is a time when people do not work or go to school.

Hippo always spends his vacation in the water.
Hippo passe toujours ses vacances dans l'eau.

VACUUM CLEANER: ASPIRATEUR

A vacuum cleaner is used to clean floors and rugs.

Piglet has a very powerful vacuum cleaner.
Cochonnet a un aspirateur très efficace.

VEGETABLES: LÉGUMES

A vegetable is an edible plant.

Carrots, peas, and cauliflowers are vegetables.
Les carottes, les petits pois, et les choux-fleurs sont des légumes.

VOLCANO: VOLCAN

A volcano is a mountain that has been formed by molten rock.

An active volcano spits fire and lava.
Un volcan en activité crache du feu et de la lave.

WAIT FOR: ATTENDRE

To wait means to stay in a place until something happens or someone comes.

Criquet is waiting for his friend Piglet.
Criquet attend son ami Cochonnet.

WAKE UP: SE REVEILLER

To wake up is to stop sleeping.

Pat always wakes up when he hears a strange noise.
Pat se réveille toujours quand il entend un bruit étrange.

WALK: MARCHER

To walk is to go somewhere on foot.

Cricket walks to school.
Criquet marche à l'école.

WALL: MUR

A wall is one side of a building or a room.

Pete the Octopus paints the wall blue.
La pieuvre Pierre peint le mur bleu.

WASH: LAVER

To wash is to clean something that is dirty.
Laver c'est nettoyer quelque chose de sale.

WATER: EAU

Water is a liquid that falls to the ground as rain.

These two ladybugs are spilling water.
Ces deux coccinelles renversent de l'eau.

WEDNESDAY: MERCREDI

Wednesday is the third day of the week.

Piglet goes to his gym every Wednesday.
Cochonnet va au gymnase tous les mercredis.

WEEK: SEMAINE

A week is made up of seven days.
Une semaine comprend sept jours.

WET: MOUILLÉ

Wet is the opposite of dry. Something wet has water or another liquid on it.

Leo the Lion has wet hair.
Le lion Léo a les cheveux mouillés.

WHALE: BALEINE

A whale is a large mammal that lives in the sea.

This whale lives in the Pacific Ocean.
Cette baleine vit dans l'océan Pacifique.

WHEEL: ROUE
A wheel is a round piece of wood, metal, or rubber that can roll.

This wheel belongs to a cart.
Cette roue appartient à une charrette.

WHERE: OÙ
We use *where* to ask a question about a place.

Where are Leo's glasses?
Où sont les lunettes de Léo?

WHICH: QUEL
We use *which* when we want to know which one.

Piglet doesn't know which cake to eat.
Cochonnet ne sait pas quel gâteau manger.

WHITE: BLANC
White is the opposite of black. It is the lightest color.

Swans and polar bears are white.
Les cygnes et les ours polaires sont blancs.

WHO: QUI

We use *who* to ask which person.

Mrs. Mouse wants to know who is at the door.
Madame Souris veut savoir qui est à la porte.

WHY: POURQUOI

We use *why* to ask the reason for something.

When we ask a question with *why*, we answer it with *because*.
Quand nous posons une question avec pourquoi, *nous répondons avec* parce que.

WIND: VENT

The wind is the air that moves over the earth.

The wind is blowing across the wheat field.
Le vent souffle à travers le champ de blé.

WINDOW: FENÊTRE

A window is an opening in a wall that lets in air and light.

The window is open.
La fenêtre est ouverte.

WINTER: HIVER

Winter is the coldest season of the year.

In winter it's very cold and it snows a lot.
En hiver il fait très froid et il neige beaucoup.

WOLF : LOUP
A wolf is a wild animal that looks like a dog.

This wolf lives alone in the woods.
Ce loup vit seul dans le bois.

WOMAN : FEMME
A woman is a grown-up female person.

Mrs. Rabbit is a very busy woman.
Madame Lapin est une femme très occupée.

WOOD : BOIS
A wood is an area with lots of trees.

There are many pine trees in this wood.
Il y a beaucoup de pins dans ce bois.

WOOL : LAINE
Wool is a fiber made from the hair of a sheep.

Tim is knitting a sweater with red wool.
Tim tricote un chandail avec de la laine rouge.

WORK: TRAVAILLER

To work is to use energy to do a job.

Porcupine works hard all day.
Porc-épic travaille dur toute la journée.

WORLD: MONDE

The world is where all people live.

Teddy's teacher shows her class a globe of the world.
La maîtresse de Teddy montre à sa classe un globe du monde.

WRITE: ÉCRIRE

To write is to put words on paper.

Teddy is writing a letter to a friend.
Teddy écrit une lettre à un ami.

YARD: JARDIN

A yard is an area next to a house or building.

Teddy's mother is planting tulips in her yard.
La maman de Teddy plante des tulipes dans son jardin.

YEAR: AN

A year is a period of twelve months.
Un an a douze mois.

YELLOW: JAUNE

Yellow is a bright color.

Lemons and bananas are yellow.
Les citrons et les bananes sont jaunes.

YES: OUI

We say "Yes" when we agree with someone.

Teddy nods his head to say "Yes."
Teddy hoche sa tête pour dire "Oui."

YOU: TU, VOUS

You refers to the person you are speaking to.
Tu, vous *indique la personne à qui on parle.*

YOUNG: JEUNE

Young means not old.

Piglet's sister is still very young.
La soeur de Cochonnet est encore très jeune.

ZEBRA: ZÈBRE

A zebra is an African animal.

Zebras look like small, striped horses.
Les zèbres ressemblent à de petits chevaux rayés.

ZERO: ZÉRO

Zero is a number that means nothing.

Zero fruits all in a row.
Zéro fruits côté à côté.

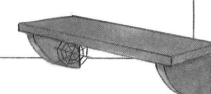

Les nombres

0 zéro

1 un

2 deux

3 trois

4 quatre

5 cinq

6 six

7 sept

8 huit

9 neuf

10 dix

11 onze

12 douze

13 treize

14 quatorze

15 quinze

16 seize

17 dix-sept

18 dix-huit

19 dix-neuf

20 vingt

126

21 vingt-et-un

22 vingt-deux

23 vingt-trois

30 trente

40 quarante

50 cinquante

60 soixante

70 soixante-dix

80 quatre-vingts

90 quatre-vingt-dix

100 cent

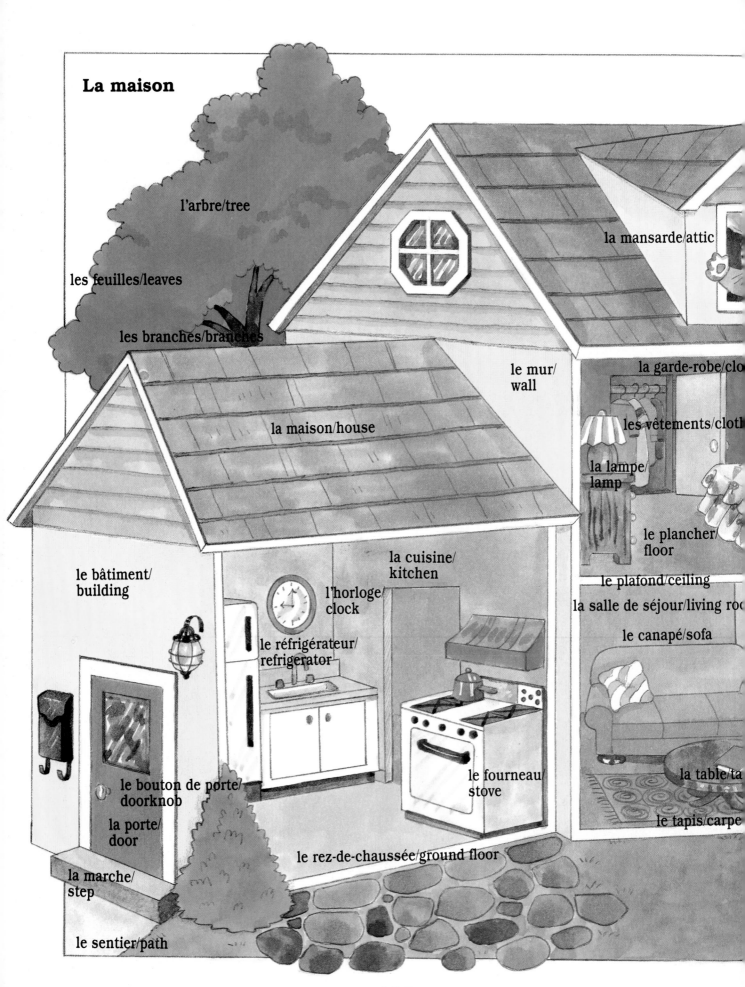

La maison

l'arbre/tree

la mansarde/attic

les feuilles/leaves

les branches/branches

le mur/
wall

la garde-robe/clo

la maison/house

les vêtements/cloth

la lampe/
lamp

le plancher/
floor

le plafond/ceiling

le bâtiment/
building

la cuisine/
kitchen

l'horloge/
clock

la salle de séjour/living ro

le canapé/sofa

le réfrigérateur/
refrigerator

le fourneau/
stove

la table/ta

le bouton de porte/
doorknob

la porte/
door

le tapis/carpe

le rez-de-chaussée/ground floor

la marche/
step

le sentier/path

128

la cheminée/chimney

les bardeaux/shingles

le toit/roof

les contrevents/shutters

la chambre/bedroom

le miroir/mirror

l'oreiller/pillow

l'évier/sink

le lit/bed

la baignoire/bathtub

la fenêtre/window

la salle de bain/bathroom

la peinture/picture

la cheminée/fireplace

le téléphone/telephone

la chaise/chair

le bureau/desk

le fauteuil/easy chair

l'herbe/grass

les fleurs/flowers

le jardin/garden

129

Les couleurs

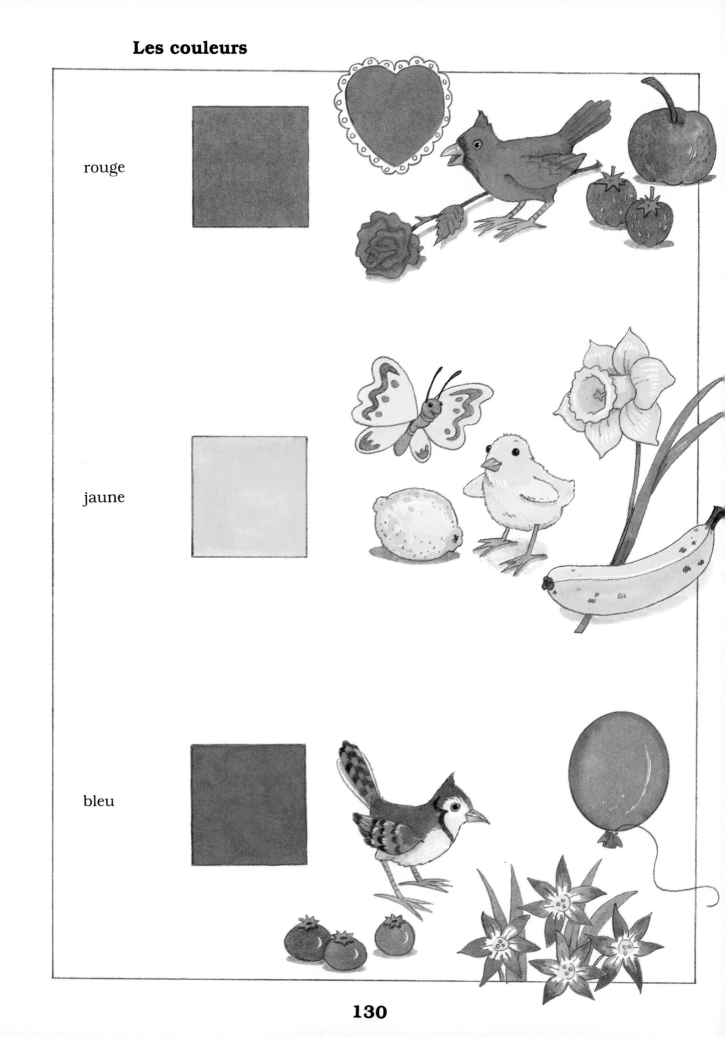

rouge

jaune

bleu

vert

orange

violet

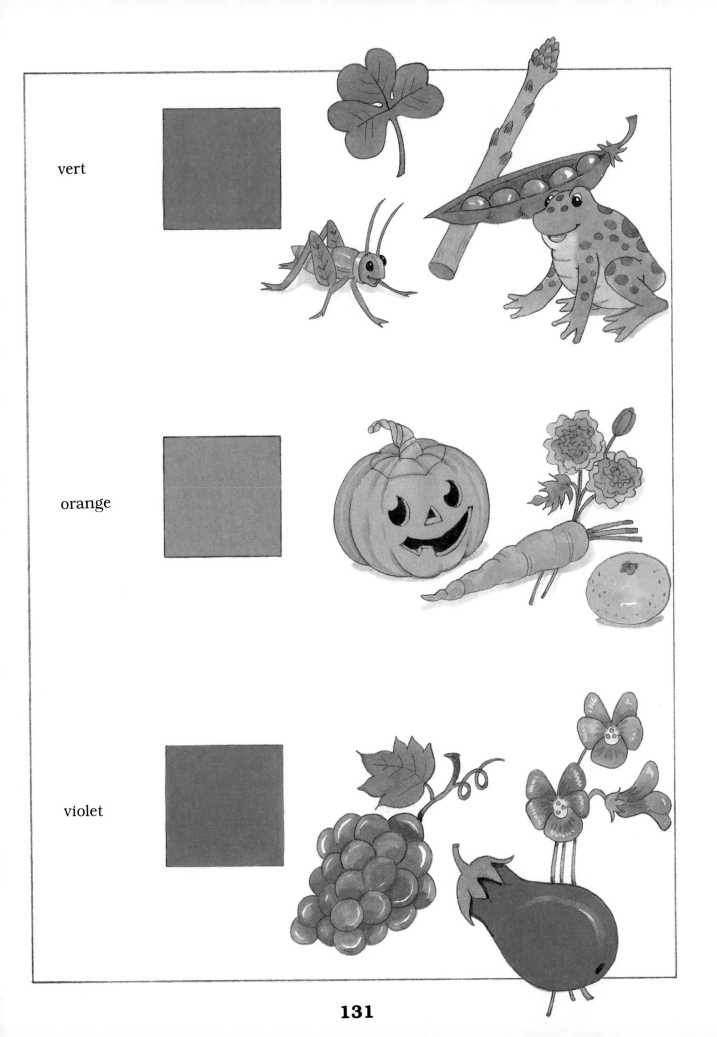

noir

brun

blanc

rose

Nationalities

américain

espagnol

arabe

français

japonaise

allemand

italien

Les formes   Shapes

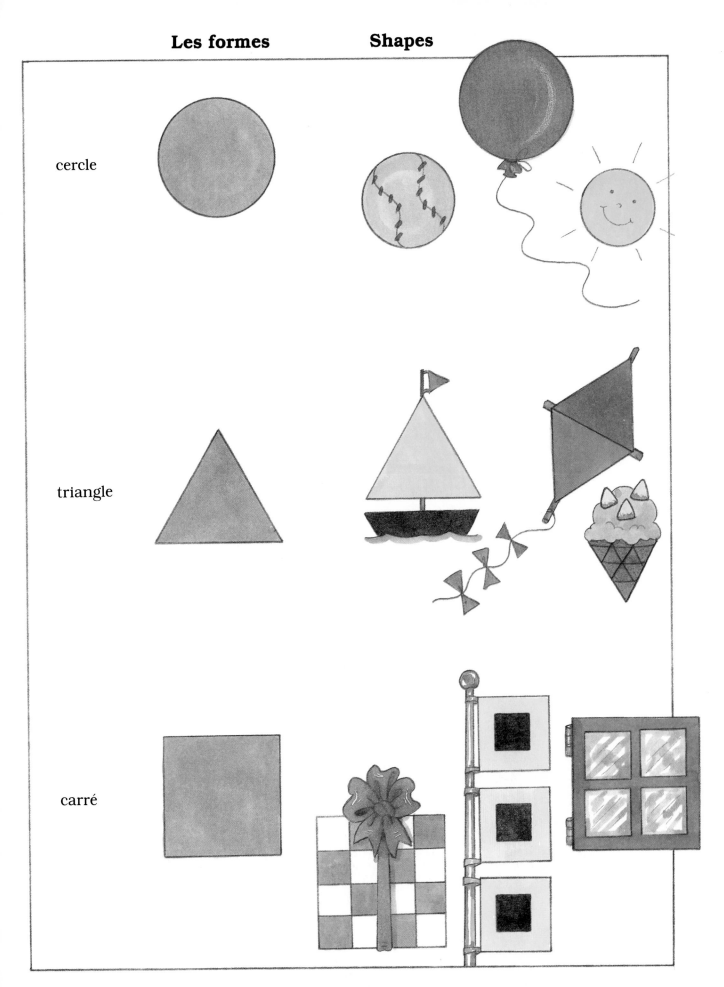

cercle

triangle

carré

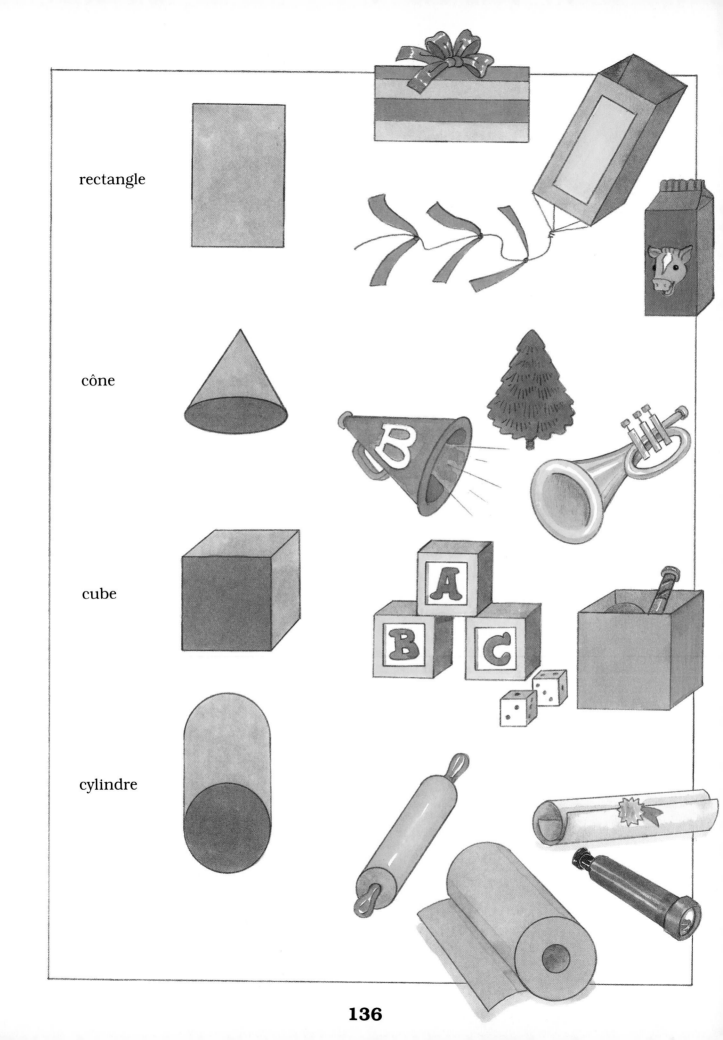

rectangle

cône

cube

cylindre

Les mois de l'année The months of the year

janvier

février

mars

avril

mai

juin

juillet

août

septembre

octobre

novembre

décembre

138

Les jours de la semaine

Monday
lundi

Tuesday
mardi

Wednesday
mercredi

Thursday
jeudi

139

Friday
vendredi

Saturday
samedi

Sunday
dimanche